ABOUT THE AUTHOR

Dr. Mark Shegelski is a full professor of physics at the University of Northern British Columbia. He loves teaching and doing research, especially with his students. His current research area is in quantum mechanics. He enjoys reading, playing eight-ball, listening to music (especially The Moody Blues, Jean Michel Jarre, and Kitaro), and watching good science fiction movies. *Remembering the Future* is his first book. He is currently writing a short novel that is based upon some of the stories in this book. He and his wife Gail live in Prince George, British Columbia, Canada.

REMEMBERING THE FUTURE

Jon, Kathy, Katie, Jenny, Jack
   Memories of good times together warm me. You've
welcomed me into your home with open arms.
   Best wishes for good reading, and all best wishes
in all ways. Love, Mark

Mark R.A. Shegelski

Mark Shegelski

Scroll Press

http://www.scrollpress.com

Library and Archives Canada
Cataloguing in Publication

Shegelski, Mark Raymond Alphonse, 1957-
Remembering the future / Mark R.A. Shegelski.

Short stories.
ISBN 978-0-9735422-5-7

I. Title.

PS8637.H447 R45 2009   C813'.6   C2009-901036-4

The paper used in this publication meets the re-
quirements of the American National Standard
for Permanence of Paper for Publications and
Documents in Libraries and Archives Z39.48 – 1992

ACKNOWLEDGEMENTS
I wish to thank those who read and commented on my stories; I cannot name you all. Many thanks to my two readers, Dr. John S. Hebron and Mr. Hal Friesen, for comments, suggestions, corrections, and more. I am grateful to Mr. Peter Thompson for a thoughtful, striking cover that captures key features of the stories, and for the skillfully executed layout. Particular thanks to my editor Dr. Dee Horne, who guided me from the start, and made sure that each story came out as well as I could make it. Special thanks to my lovely wife Gail, without whom this book would not be.

Contents

THE QUIET ROOM

\\\

It all started off so well. I used the room to help me get my work done. I didn't realize at first what was happening, and when I did, I thought only of how it could benefit me. I would have eventually used it to help others, but it's too late for that now. I might never be able to go back to the way things used to be.

All I wanted was a quiet place to live near the university where I could work in peace and not be disturbed. Looking back, I was obsessed with having privacy to do my studies, and that was the reason I rented the place. In the suite was a room at the back that was quiet. Utterly silent. The room had no windows, and had heavy insulation all around the walls, the ceiling, the floor, and the single door, with the lock on the outside still in place. Horrible things had happened in this room. I don't even want to think about that, and I am sure that no one else would have even considered staying here. The lock on the outside of the door gave me the creeps. It would have to go.

I approached the landlord and we worked out a deal. I could use the suite and, more importantly, the quiet room.

Being in that room was like being cut off from the world. Perhaps that's why all of this happened.

I remember when I first understood what was going on. I was overwhelmed then, I'll admit it. But I was also delighted, and captivated. I had something special. I could use it. And I did.

The first time it happened was the day Portier gave out the first assignment. She'd warned us that it would be very difficult, that there was no room in her course for any but the best. We'd do well just to finish the assignment, never mind finishing it on time.

"Just get as far as you can, and hand in what you have done by next class," she'd said, raising her hand and sweeping it through the air in front of her.

I loved a good challenge. After reading the assignment and getting some materials that might help, I was ready to head home and to the quiet room. Then I remembered that Kitt and I had plans for the evening. I wanted to get right to the assignment, but didn't want to break our plans. We'd agreed to meet at the library.

As I approached the library, I saw Kitt Daniels sitting on the steps. Her attention was on a book she was reading. I slowed my pace and stopped. She had long, straight, black hair with bangs down to her eyebrows. The sunlight reflected off her hair, giving it a shimmering, blue-black color. She nodded and smiled slightly as she took in whatever she was reading. Suddenly her eyes lifted from the book and looked into mine. She held me with her gaze, quickly blinking a couple of times. Her lips carried a subtle smile, as if she had secret thoughts of me.

"Hi," I said and sat beside her.

She leaned over to kiss me lightly on my cheek.

2

"How was your first day?" I asked.

"Fine. My archeology courses sound great. I'm really looking forward to them. How about you? How was your quantum mechanics class?"

"It's started with a blast. Portier's given us a really tough assignment." I raised my eyebrows and rubbed the back of my hand across my forehead. "She wants to separate the brilliant from the merely very smart."

"How long do you have to do it?"

"It's due next class."

Kitt put her hand on my arm. "On Friday? So you only have two days?"

"Two days."

She gently squeezed my arm. "Let's put our plans on hold. We can go bowling on the weekend," she suggested.

"No, no. It's all right. Let's go now." I stood up.

But Kitt didn't get up. She drummed her fingers on the step beside her. "I can tell you really want to get to this assignment, John. It's all right. We can wait until Friday or Saturday." She looked up at me and smiled.

I tilted my head to the side, pressed my lips together, and nodded slightly. "You're amazing, Kitt. The weekend it is."

I reached out. Kitt placed her hands in mine, and I pulled her up. We hugged and I whispered my thanks to her. Kitt kissed me feather light on the cheek, and wished me luck.

Having put off going out with Kitt, I was even more determined to solve the problem. As soon as I got home, I went to the quiet room. I wanted to plunge

3

right into the assignment, but I had trouble getting started. Something was not quite right. I looked around the room and knew what it was. I had to close the door, had to have that feeling of total isolation.

I returned to my desk, sat down, and started thinking. It didn't take long for me to realize just how challenging an assignment it was, and some doubt crept into my mind. I started my calculations. I thought through the ideas that came to me, progressing steadily, carefully, going slow enough to make sure not to make any errors, fast enough to keep the ideas flowing. The problem had subtleties, and I enjoyed weaving through them. Not long into my work, excited by the challenge, a tingling sensation passed through my body, and the world dissolved around me. While solving the problem, I was so deeply engrossed that I knew nothing but the ideas, the thoughts. Later, I would remember nothing but my thinking. It was as if I had not sat on the chair, placed my arms on the desk, or held the pencil in my hand. Suddenly, I was finished and I was numb all over. I emerged from a trance-like state of mind. At first, everything I saw was blurry. I had difficulty focusing my eyes, and I blinked several times. Slowly, fuzzy shapes took form and I was again aware of the room around me. I leaned back into the chair. I lifted my arms and hands and inspected them as if seeing them for the first time. I'd never before been so deep into thought, and it seemed like I was awakening from a deep sleep.

It's hard to say how long I was at it. Several hours at least. I had the answer, and it checked out. Satisfied that I'd done it correctly, I decided it was time to eat something. Then I remembered: I'd put a pot of beans on the stove before I'd started working, and by now they would be burned to black soot. I expected there to be smoke in the suite. I rushed to the door and opened it and ... no odor, nothing.

I ran to the kitchen and found that the pot of beans wasn't even bubbling. I took the pot off and saw that the element wasn't hot. Waving my hand over it, I found that the heating had barely just begun. Strange, I thought. It must not have clicked on when I'd set it, and somehow had just come on now.

I checked the time. It was 7:11. My watch must have stopped. I remembered that it was 7:11 when I'd started the assignment; I tend to remember primes and lucky numbers, so I was certain. Then I saw that the clock on the stove also read 7:11. I brought my watch to my ear and heard the soft ticking. That was pretty weird, but obviously I had worked twelve hours, almost to the minute. It didn't feel like so much time had gone by, but then again, time is a subjective thing, and I had done a lot of work. I looked out the kitchen window. It was light outside, so I knew that I had, indeed, worked for twelve hours.

After eating, I wrote up the assignment neatly. Then I decided to sleep for a couple of hours. As I closed the blinds in my bedroom, I noticed that it was a bit darker outside. It had clouded over, just as the weather forecast had predicted. I set my alarm for 9:45 a.m. and at maximum volume because I don't wake easily. I wanted to be on time for my 10:30 Thursday class.

I fell into a deep sleep, woke to the alarm, showered, and headed up to the university. Before the class, I met some of the other students and they were talking about the assignment question. Some of them had worked all night and hadn't put a dent in it, and I'll admit that I enjoyed some satisfaction upon hearing this.

After my 10:30 class I went to Professor Portier's office. I found the door open and her inside, working. I knocked quietly on the door. She glanced up at me, barely moving her head. Her gaze fell back on the paper in front of her, and she wrote quickly for a moment. She gently placed her pen down, said "Hello," and directed me into her office with a wave of her hand.

"Hello, Professor Portier."

She placed her hands palms down on her desk, nodding slightly.

"I'm in your quantum mechanics class. My name is John Meyers."

"What can I do for you, Mr. Meyers?" she asked.

"I've done the assignment and I wondered if I could hand it in early?"

She raised her eyebrows and actually laughed. "You're done? Already?"

I had hoped she'd be impressed. I swallowed and nodded quickly. "Yes," I said, more forcefully, "I am done, and done early, and I think my answer is correct."

Maybe I'd said too much. She stared at me, shaking her head slightly. "You're done? Your answer is correct?"

She stood, placed her knuckles on her desk, and

leaned forward. I almost stepped back as she squinted and asked, "What was your result?"

I told her.

Her eyes widened. "How did you find the answer?" she said sharply.

I feared she thought I had cheated.

My fingers twitched. "I worked very carefully, Professor Portier. I didn't rush and I kept a steady pace." I explained the steps I'd made.

Every now and then she asked a question, and my answers seemed to satisfy her. She asked for my assignment, sat back down, and started to read it. Now and then, she would purse her lips, shake her head slightly, and mumble to herself. Her frown grew deeper with each page she read.

I had been so sure I had done it correctly. I rubbed the back of my hand over my forehead as I wondered where I had gone wrong. I couldn't think of anything.

Finally, she reached the end. She closed the assignment and tossed it on her desk.

"Mr. Meyers," she said, "I will come straight to it." She again rose, put her hands on her desk, moved her head toward me until her eyes were only inches from mine, and asserted, rather than asked, "You cheated."

I stammered. "Yes, it's my— I mean: no, I didn't cheat. It's my own work."

She was quiet. She waited.

I was sweating.

Her phone rang. She ignored it.

She said, "If you have done this work yourself, you have done a truly spectacular job."

Why did she doubt me? I'd done it, after all. So it couldn't have been so spectacular a thing that I'd gotten it right. Sure, I'm a smart person, but no way am I in the brilliant-beyond-belief category.

"Mr. Meyers. Can you do another problem this difficult, overnight?"

I hesitated and she added, "Not tonight, next week. Can you do it?"

I understood. I had no choice.

"Yes, I think so. But I'm not sure if I can do it on top of my regular assignments."

"You won't have to," she said. Whispering, she explained, "I'll give you a different assignment next week, a question more challenging than the one I will give to the rest of the class." She sat down. "I always give a very difficult assignment at the beginning of my courses. That way the students know I mean business." She leaned forward. "The assignment I will give to the class next week will be easy compared to the one you've just done." She paused. "I expect that you realize this is confidential, Mr. Meyers."

"Of course," I reassured her, and put my hand in my pocket.

She waved me out of her office.

I turned to leave, but then stopped.

"Is there something else, Mr. Meyers?" she asked briskly.

"Ah, it's just ... did I solve the problem correctly?"

"What you wrote is most certainly correct. See you in class tomorrow," she said, nodding toward the door.

8

* * *

Friday evening, Kitt and I went bowling. We played mostly just the two of us, but also had a few games with a couple of Kitt's friends. One of them flirted subtly with me. I ignored it and she soon stopped.

Afterwards, we went to Kitt's for a snack. We talked about the bowling and our courses and other things. After a while we fell silent. Kitt tapped a finger on her lips. Something was on her mind, and I thought I knew what it was.

"It bothered me that your friend would flirt like that right in front of you."

"So you noticed?"

"Of course." I opened my hands. I quickly added, "But I paid no attention to her, and she quit, so…"

She was silent for a moment, then, looking down, she said, "You could have mentioned this earlier you know."

"I know. I discouraged her, so it didn't seem important to talk about."

She slapped her hand on her thigh. "It's important to me. I'd rather you told me sooner. Suppose I hadn't noticed. Then it would be like you had something to hide."

"Kitt, I have nothing to hide. You know what you mean to me."

We talked more about it until the tension eased up.

* * *

The beginning of the next week dragged by. The assignments I got in my other courses were much easier

9

than the one Portier had given us. I spent only a little time in my quiet room, working slowly but steadily, getting the assignments done quickly, and learning the material in the other classes.

Finally, Wednesday came and Portier gave the class the second assignment. "This one's going to be easy," she quipped as she looked directly at me. After class I went up to the front to get 'my' second assignment. She pulled it from a folder and slid it into my hand.

As I read it, I dragged my hand across my brow. I read it a second time. A third time. This was a monster of a question. I didn't even fully understand it. I asked her some questions. Time ran out and another class came in the room. We went to her office.

She answered all my questions and explained the problem fully. It most definitely was a huge question.

Was this the end for me? A week into graduate school?

No. I would do it. Somehow, I would figure it out. I feared what Portier might think if I didn't get this question right too.

I went straight home, to the quiet room in my suite. I decided to skip supper, eat when I was done. No matter how long it took. I would work until I solved the problem. I slipped my watch over my hand and put it in my bag. I pulled out the assignment and a stack of paper and plenty of pencils and erasers. After closing the door, I set to work.

It was slow going at first. I thought about a number of approaches. I noticed that there was a symmetry I could use to solve the puzzle. That got me fully into the problem. Again the tingling descended upon me, and I plunged into a world where only my thoughts and ideas existed. I worked methodically, taking no short-cuts and doing all the calculations in full. I worked a long time. There were a few occasions when I thought I was beaten, but each time I persevered and found a new path. I followed them all, and eventually had the problem done.

The room around me was fuzzy. I had to close and open my eyes slowly a few times before I was able to perceive the details of the room, somewhat like when you reach your destination after driving and you wonder how you got there.

Did I have time to write it up neatly? I pulled out my watch and saw that it was 6:55. My watch doesn't indicate a.m. or p.m. This assignment had been harder than the first one, and I had probably spent twice as long on this one. Did that mean it was 6:55, Thursday night? I hadn't noticed exactly what time I'd started, but it had to have been about 6 or 7 o'clock when I'd gotten home Wednesday evening. I realized that I'd missed my Thursday classes, but it was worth finishing the assignment.

I'd done it. I closed my hand into a fist, pumped upward, and shouted a triumphant "Yes." I still had plenty of time to write it up neatly and hand it in. It wasn't due until the next class, which would be to-morrow. The thrill of success and a wonderful sense of relief warmed me. Strangely, I wasn't very tired. I checked the steps as I wrote and I was satisfied I had gotten this one right too.

After eating and taking a shower, I flopped out on my bed. Suddenly I remembered that Professor Portier had asked me if I could do another difficult problem "overnight!" That meant that the assignment was due today.

I glanced at my watch. It was about 10 p.m., not too late. Professor Portier was known to be at the university from early morning to almost midnight, so there was a good chance she'd still be there. I sprang off the bed, dressed, and hurried to the university.

I was out of breath when I reached her door. I didn't need to knock. Her door was open and no doubt she'd heard my panting. She smiled and said, "Do you need some help, Mr. Meyers? This problem a bit too much? Or have you not yet started?"

What was she saying? I wouldn't wait twenty-four hours to start the assignment. I tilted my head to the side and said, "I've not only started, I've finished."

"What? Impossible."

"But I am done. You asked if I could do it overnight. If anything, I'm late because it's taken me about..." I checked my watch, "... about twenty-nine hours."

"Whatever are you talking about, Mr. Meyers? It was only late this afternoon that you got the assignment." She paused, and then said, "All right. I see. I suppose you are saying that it seems like it's been twenty-nine hours ... *to you*." Her eyes narrowed. "But that ... Are you saying that you've done it in ... in..." She glanced at the time on her computer screen. "In less than five hours?"

If it was Wednesday night, I'd somehow done the

problem in about five hours. No. Less than that. Three hours. There was no way that I could have done so. I'd felt sure that I'd worked much more than three hours. Just writing the assignment up had taken about an hour. But I couldn't go back and say I wasn't done.

My thoughts were buzzing. My fingers twitched. I dropped my assignment and picked it back up. What was wrong with me? How could I think that I'd worked so long when it was really just a few hours? Yet how could I have done the work I had in such a short time? The problem was much too difficult to solve in two or three hours. No wonder she'd been suspicious.

I mulled over what had been going on in the quiet room. Could the answer be in that room? How? I was baffled.

I didn't get a chance to think much about it then, because she walked quickly over to me and took the assignment from my hand.

She started to read it. Slowly at first. Then she made her way to her desk, sat, continued to read it. The more she read, the deeper she frowned. Now and then, she pursed her lips and shook her head abruptly, side to side.

Had it really been only five hours since I'd gotten the assignment? That had to be it; it had seemed so much longer than that. I ran my hand up and down my right cheek. Time is subjective, I reminded myself. What had felt like ten or twenty hours to me must have actually just been a few hours. Now, as I waited for her to finish reading my work, my impression was again that a very long time went by, an hour maybe, but she finished reading in just fifteen minutes. So that explained everything. There was no big mystery here. I must have misread my watch, and misjudged the amount of time that had passed. At least, that's what I believed at that moment. What Professor Portier would say next would change that.

"Do you have any idea what you have done?" she asked.

"I haven't done anything," I protested. "I've simply solved the problem you gave me. No cheating."

"No, that's not what I mean. I know you didn't cheat."

"You know I didn't cheat," I repeated, quietly. Then I asked how she knew.

"This problem that I gave you? Do you know where you can find the answer?"

"Well," I said in a small voice, "the correct answer is in my assignment, right?"

She smiled, but only slightly. "Where else?"

Then I understood, or thought I did. "Are you saying that you, and you alone, have solved this problem? That it's not on-line or published anywhere?"

"More than that, Mr. Meyers. This problem had not yet been solved when I gave it to you this afternoon. It has only been asked *just today*." She rapped her knuckles on the desk.

My mouth fell open and I froze.

"That's right. I made this problem up this morning. I've thought of problems like this one, but this particular one has not been looked at." She shook a finger in the air. "Or, it hadn't been. Not until you solved it today. And you did get the correct answer, as far as I can see." Her right hand shuffled some articles on her desk.

"I wanted a problem that I could know you'd have to have solved on your own," she said, as she stood and walked toward me. "I have to tell you: I'm impressed. I didn't think you could do the problem. And so quickly." She shook her head. "But every step in your assignment is correct, as far as I can see, and the final answer makes sense. So you have done it correctly, and in a very short time."

"I hardly noticed the time," I said.

"While I'm at it, I'll be honest: I want you as my grad student. So will all the other professors, when they find out how good you are."

I rubbed my cheek and scratched my neck, trying to absorb all of this.

"Well? Yes or no? Or do you need more time?"

"Yes. I mean, no." I stopped, drew in a single, deep breath, and slowly said, "I mean, yes I'll be glad to be your grad student, and no I don't need more time."

We shook hands and exchanged smiles, mine forced and awkward.

I should have felt a thrill like none I'd had in a very long time: I would be working with the famous Professor Portier. But I was so upset I only wanted to go somewhere and figure everything out.

I'm not sure exactly what I did next. I walked around campus, went to the graduate student center, checked the time. I remember that Jack Renard and Phil Billings were playing snooker. "Hey, guys," I said, "is the football game two days from now, Friday night, or is it on Saturday?"

Phil broke his gaze from a shot he was lining up, laughed quietly, and said, "Well, you know John, usually two days after Wednesday is Friday, so, yeah, that would mean the game is on Friday."

I shrugged and went away, satisfied. I didn't realize that the nightmare was well underway.

I went back home and sat for a long time, thinking. An idea came to mind. I checked the time on the kitchen clock and on my watch. I slipped my watch off and left it on the kitchen table. After a few slow, deep breaths, I wrote down the time and went to the quiet room with one of my assignments. I closed the door, sat down, focused on the questions, worked my way through the assignment, and wrote it up in good. I estimated that I had worked for at least an hour and a half. Then I took my assignment with me and left the room. I checked my watch and the time on the kitchen clock.

They still read the same time as when I'd entered the room. Was I going crazy? I thought so, at first. In the days and weeks to follow, I tested this room, tried out a lot of different ideas, and did some experiments. When I had finished, I knew the rules.

When I worked in that room, with the door closed, lost in thought and isolated from the rest of the world, I'd be very productive, yet no time would pass outside the room. I would not grow weary, or sleepy. I would not get hungry or thirsty or need to relieve myself. It was as if time had been frozen.

If I stopped working and became aware of my surroundings, then, even if the door was shut, I *would* get hungry and thirsty, and I would tire. Time would pass for me, but still *no time would go by outside the room.*

I thought I had something wonderful, a place to go and work and get things done with no need to worry about how long it took. I knew this was precious and I decided that I must never allow anyone to know what I had, not even Kitt.

I was moving to the future much more slowly than people outside the quiet room. That reminded me of a conversation Kitt and I had when we first met. We'd each represented our schools in the city's high school chess tournament, ending up competing in the championship match. The game had been close. I had squeaked out a win, but couldn't bear the idea of not seeing her again. Fortunately, she'd agreed to have coffee with me.

"Besides winning more chess championships," I asked her, "what do you plan to do after graduation?"

"Archeology," she replied.

"Ah, 'Kitt Daniels and the Raiders of the Lost Ark,'" I said.

"Not so crazy as that." She laughed. "What about you?"

"Physics." I tried to think of something to say. "Did you know that 'Raiders of the Lost Ark' is a remake of an earlier movie? The first one came out in the 1980s."

"I didn't know that. Was the first movie good?"

"Actually not bad at all, but there was no time travel in it."

"I've got a question for you. How did Indiana Jones

17

move so quickly through time? You know, in that scene where he's being chased, runs into the mist, and comes out one day later?"

"And Belloq is foiled again, Jones having vanished from him."

"Right."

"You can't go through time like that, but there are other ways to do it."

"How?" she asked.

"Well, one way is to travel near the speed of light, away from Earth, slow down, turn around, and speed back. You'd have only one month go by, maybe, but Earth would have gone many years into the future, so you'd have traveled quickly to the future like Jones did."

"I remember that, about traveling fast away from Earth, now that you've pointed it out."

"There's another way to go to the future quickly. You leave Earth and go to a star with huge gravity. You orbit around it for a while and return to Earth. Again, a month goes by for you but Earth goes through a few years."

Thinking back on that made me ask myself, why can't you do the opposite? Why couldn't you go to the future much more *slowly* than everybody else? That's exactly what I was doing in the quiet room. Outside the room one minute would go by, but inside the room it would take me much longer to get to that next minute. There must be some reason why I was travelling slowly to the future. Nothing in the physics I knew said that this was impossible. It was happening, for me, every time I was lost in thought inside the quiet room.

I've thought of a possible explanation.

In quantum mechanics, the role of a conscious observer is very important. Could it be that, when I was in that room, my consciousness was so isolated that I was cut off from the outside world? Time for me was different than time outside the room? Nobody understands time, not really, and no one knows how to treat it in a proper way in quantum mechanics. For physical things that can be observed there are mathematical operations, or 'operators,' in quantum mechanics. Time is a very important exception. There is no operator for time. Maybe that is somehow linked to how the future advances slowly in the quiet room.

Regardless, I now knew the rules of the quiet room. Thinking back on it, whenever I finished working in that room, I would recall only the thoughts and ideas I had while doing the work and nothing else. Perhaps the state of my conscious mind determined whether or not time would pass for me after all.

Over the rest of the fall term, I used the room to do all my assignments and to learn all the material presented in the lectures. It took me almost no time at all. So I never bothered to do much work up at the university. That was a mistake. People began to notice. I became the guy who was never seen working yet always had assignments done and understood all the topics in all the courses. I even got most of my research done for my Master's thesis in record time, thanks to the quiet room.

My fellow students started to wonder about me. They'd ask, "Why are you such a slow worker here, John, and yet you get so much done at home?"

"You guys are always bugging me, wanting to shoot snooker. Drink beer. At home, I just do my work." They didn't look convinced. "I focus better at home," I explained, "when I'm alone and it's quiet."

Word got around. I knew it wouldn't be long until Kitt heard about it. She'd ask me questions that I wouldn't want to answer. It happened the day after lectures ended.

We were at my place. We'd just played tennis and were cooling down, sipping our water.

"What is this stuff about you working at the speed of light?" she asked, suddenly.

I coughed. "What do you mean?"

"People say you never do any work at the university, that you do it all at home."

"So what's wrong with that?" I asked her.

"Nothing. Just..." She tapped her fingernail on her cup.

"Just what?"

"You're different John. You don't seem yourself somehow. What's wrong?"

I wasn't sure what to say. I knew she had sensed that there was more to this. "Nothing is wrong," I said. "I'm the same person I've always been. It's just that ... just that I..."

I wondered if this was the right time to tell her more about the room. She'd seen it before, of course, but I had always steered the discussion onto another topic.

20

Now, as we talked, we made our way to the room. I sat in the chair and she sat, facing me, on the top of the desk, the door behind her and on my right.

"This," I waved my hand in the air, "is the room."

"Is there something special about this room?" she asked. "Do you work better in here?"

I hesitated. What should I tell her? I couldn't expect her to believe what had happened to me in here.

"There is something, I can tell, John. What is it?"

"You'd never believe it." As soon as the words came out of my mouth, I wanted to take them back.

"You don't know that! Tell me. I'll decide if I believe it." She looked down into her cup. "You should be able to trust me, to be honest with me," she said. "You've never talked to me about this room, and now you're holding something back."

I shrugged.

She slid off the desk and put down her cup with a loud thud. This time, she spoke sharply. "You used to trust me before. Why not now? What's different?"

When I didn't reply, she crossed her arms, and placed her hand over her mouth. She shook her head, turned around, and slammed the door as she left the room.

I sat there a while, trying to figure out what to say, how to make things better. I thought for a long time about telling her the whole story. Eventually, I decided that this would be the right thing to do.

I got up, walked to the door, and turned the handle.

I couldn't open the door! I twisted the handle and

pulled on the door. Still it didn't budge. I rattled the handle and yanked on the door again. I pounded on the door. "Kitt," I screamed, "come back!" I couldn't breathe. Feeling dizzy, I sat down on the floor.

Calm down, I told myself. She'll come back. She'll open the door. Just wait a bit.

* * *

I have been in here for what seems like forever. On the other side of the door, Kitt has just finished locking it, and it's only a matter of time until she'll come back and open it. It might take her ten minutes, or maybe an hour, or more. No matter how quickly she comes back, it's going to be much too long for me.

That first time, when I'd put the pot of beans on the stove, almost no time passed outside the room. The element had only just begun to warm. It could be an eternity for me before the door would open again. I shudder at the possibility that the door was shut and locked at almost the same time. I shake my head at the thought that she might leave, might forget that she locked the door.

I wish I'd told her about this room, told her from the very beginning. I wish I'd removed the lock.

I'm trying to keep my mind occupied by working out problems, whatever I can think of. It's hard to keep this up. It's easy to fall out of this state of mind. When I do, I feel the time going by, and I know I can only last so long.

THE MIND WIPE

\\\

Pender leaned toward me, tilted his forehead, and lifted his bushy eyebrows. "Do you want the job or not?"

What choice did I have? I brought the heels of my palms up to my forehead. "Yes," I said, and dropped my arms.

"Then let's get on with it. Are you ready, Jack-o?" he asked me.

I slowly sat down on the chair, slid my legs onto the leg-rest, and glanced up at Pender. He snapped his fingers, *snap-snap-snap.* "Come on Jack-o, let's go." I placed my hands next to my hips and pushed myself rearward, letting my back and shoulders sink into the chair. It adjusted its shape until I had maximum comfort and my sense of touch was gone. Pender attached wires to various spots on my head and fitted the sensory pad over my face, ears, and neck. Within a few seconds I was there.

It was too perfect to be true. Cars crept along the congested lanes. Horns honked. The walk light changed and beeped, and I crossed the road. I rubbed my hands together. My fingers gently touched my cheeks. I blinked. Blinked again. It had to be real, I thought, though I knew better.

"Just a simulation," Pender had said.

Just. No, not just. What I was experiencing was the same as if it actually existed. A simulacrum, created by Pender. "Why?" I had asked him.

"To prepare you, train you. For the true task."

He would not tell me what that was, but I knew it was something that most people wouldn't do, couldn't do. How had he found me? My past was supposed to have been cleansed. The partial mind wipe had been good enough to let me slip back into society. The wipe was supposed to have removed *all* memories of what I'd done and of all events and experiences that had made me do it. But some recollections remained.

I thought of one time when I had asked my wife, Janice, "Do you remember any of it?" Her hair was shoulder length, wavy, a mix of blond and brown with a touch of red. She'd worn a peach top that accentuated the red in her hair.

She had breathed in deeply before replying. "I told you Jack: I don't want to talk about it."

"But it's all gone from you."

"Yes, it is, and I don't want to do anything that might ruin it."

"But I *do* remember. Parts of it. I need to talk about it, Janice."

She'd hesitated, mouth open, and her eyes had darted about the room.

"I'm so sorry, Jack." She placed the back of her hand on her forehead and closed her eyes. Then she hugged me. "I can't. I'm afraid that it might make me remember what *I* did."

24

Pender had to know. That was why he'd picked me. He believed, I think, that if I could recall a little of what I had done, perhaps I could do what he was paying me to do. No doubt he knew about Janice's history too, but her wipe had been complete, so she wasn't eligible. I had that much to be thankful for.

Pender needed me. I suppose I needed Pender too, or the money, anyway.

Standing at the street corner, I told myself that, yes, I could do it. It was, after all, an imaginary city. I made my way into the building and to the man's office, opened his door, walked in, and closed it behind me. Everything was precisely where Pender had said it would be.

The man looked up at me. "What are you doing in here? Who are you?"

"Quiet," I said, and touched a finger to my lips, glancing behind me. I walked quickly to his side and he swiveled his chair to face me.

He was frowning. "What's going on?" he asked.

With no hesitation I slapped his face as hard as I could.

My eyes widened. My mouth fell open. It was as before, not as intense perhaps, but the taste was the same. I don't like admitting it, but I was, at that moment, pleased that the mind wipe hadn't quite erased everything.

His jaw dropped, but no words came out. His hand slowly rose toward his bright red cheek.

I slapped his other cheek and reacted the same as before.

25

I gritted my teeth, and pulled at bunches of my hair with my hands. "It's only a simulation," I whispered, repeating what Pender had told me a dozen times.

Without warning I was back. The facial pad was removed, the wires pulled off me.

"Good enough for now, Jack-o," said Pender.

I got up and put out my hand. "My payment," I demanded.

He reached into his pocket and pulled out a wad of money. He rolled the elastic band off the bundle and then, holding one end between his thumb and forefinger, flapped the bills through the air.

"Here's your money, Jack-o," he said, and eased the greenbacks toward me until they were within my reach.

I forced myself not to snatch my earnings from him. When I squeezed the end of the stack he gripped the bills tighter. When I pulled a bit harder, so did Pender. He suddenly let them go, and I rocked backward as they came into my grasp.

"Tomorrow, Jack-o. Round two," he said.

* * *

Later, when Janice and I were in bed, she asked, "What is this job?"

"It's a ... computer generated place."

"What do you mean?"

I cleared my throat.

"You can't tell anyone."

"You know I won't," she protested.

"All right. He's training me for something. He gave me my first job today." I explained about the wires

26

and the illusory city. "When I was there, I did what he wanted."

"Who?"

I sat up, but said nothing.

"What did you do?"

"Janice, I can't tell you that."

"Why not?"

"It concerns what you never want to mention. It's about my mind wipe not quite being complete. So he picked me. He must know somehow."

"No, Jack, no. Tell me you didn't do…"

I took a deep breath and let it out slowly. "It's not what you think. I slapped a guy, that's all. It's all made up," I said. "Nobody's getting hurt."

She sat up and laid her hand on my chest. "*You're* getting hurt, Jack, if it's leading you to do what you did before." Her fingers touched my cheek, and she added, "Please. Don't do it anymore."

Inwardly, I knew it wasn't going to be limited to slapping. Still, I said, "I have to, Janice. We both know how hard it is for you to get work. You're at minimum wage. People don't treat us right. They all seem to know about us. You have trouble even though your mind wipe was complete." I shook my head and pulled at my hair. I put my elbows on my thighs and lowered the tops of my eye sockets onto the balls of my thumbs. I closed my eyes. "Somehow, everyone knows all about me."

"How could they know, Jack?"

"I don't know. But they do."

I reached out and took her in my arms. "I have to keep this job."

Janice said nothing.

"I'll do things only in this fake world, Janice. I promise."

She took my face in her hands and kissed me gently on the lips. "Be careful, Jack."

Later, while Janice slept, I thought about what I'd done. What would be next?

* * *

I did what Pender asked. The tasks escalated. I knew they would, but even so, each time I left the simulated realm, I shuddered. Each time, it took longer to get past what I'd done. "None of this exists," I kept telling myself, but that wasn't enough to prevent me from going further down the path Pender had put me on.

* * *

"This is the last simulation, Jack-o. Tomorrow you do the real work."

I nodded and started toward the chair.

"No, Jack-o," Pender said. "Over here today." He directed me to a different chair. I hadn't noticed it before.

"There are no connections," I pointed out.

"It's an improved system." He snapped his fingers, three times, quickly. "Let's get started." He went to a closet and pulled out a clear, plastic garment. "Put this on," he said and handed it to me.

"This is going to be in the simulation?"

"Yes."

28

"So why do I need it?"

"This has to be as realistic as possible. Your last task is crucial, and you'll need this suit to do it. What you do now has to seem as real as possible. In fact … what you're doing today will start with you in this room, sitting exactly the same way. You won't even notice that you've gone from here to the fabricated world. You'll blink and I'll be gone. You'll be sitting here, and your target will be standing over there examining the computer monitor." He pointed. "You take him out."

I didn't believe I could do it, not even in a simulation.

"You'll need that garb tomorrow, so that any evidence will be on the outside of it. Then, after it's over, the suit and everything on it will be destroyed. No trail back to you, Jack-o, and more importantly, no connection to me."

This was it: the last time before 'the final job,' or so he thought. Pender didn't need to know that this day would be the last time I'd come to his lab.

I put on the garment and the specialized plastic molded itself to fit my body snugly. As it closed over my head and face, I smelled a foul odor and was briefly claustrophobic while openings formed for my eyes, ears, nose, and mouth. The odor faded. I sat. Pender pulled down a hemisphere from the ceiling. It surrounded my head from my forehead down to my chin. It seemed to be made of glass, with many copper wires strung through it in a checkerboard pattern.

"Ready Jack-o?"

"Yes."

"Close your eyes."

"I—"

"Do it!" he shouted as he raised his right hand, his fist shaking.

I waited until he lowered his arm, and then complied. I heard the rustling of his coat and the clicking of switches. My eyelids widened to slits, and I watched him going through the final few steps. I peeked out and saw Pender vanish.

My target was hunched over the monitor.

I sat up and he turned around. He was much smaller than I, and I knew what his fate would be.

"Who are you? What...? Why are you wearing...? Stay away from me!"

But it was much too late for him. I had closed the gap. I was surprised to find my hands around his throat. As if in a dream, they squeezed, closing off his windpipe, and his face twisted as I raised him off the floor.

My skin tingled. I grinned and grimaced at the same time, my hands pressing on the man's neck.

He went limp, but my hands would not relax. After a moment I dropped him to the floor.

I'd done it. It left me numb. It couldn't have turned out any other way, I realized. I wished I'd listened to Janice...

"Nicely done, Jacky boy."

Pender!

"What are you doing here? Why are you in the simulation?"

He grinned. "Pretty realistic, huh?"

"Yeah. Way too much."

He raised his arms, and twirled in a full circle.

"How do I look, Jacky boy? Believable enough for you?"

I nodded. "Why are you here?"

"Can't tell it from the real thing, right?" He chuckled and threw his head back. "Know why?"

I looked at the dead body.

He followed my glance and laughed. "Because it *is* real. *You're not in any simulation*, Jacky boy! That's a man you killed. You're a murderer." He paused, and then said it, as I knew he would. "Again."

"No. No way." I thought about what had happened, pointed a limp finger at him, and said, "That can't be, Pender. You weren't here ... and that guy was." My eyes moved to the lifeless body. "That couldn't have happened in ... in the time that I..."

"That's why I told you to close your eyes. Had to make sure you'd see me vanish and the other guy come out of nowhere. By the way, Jacky boy, you're making a mistake," he taunted. "You're assuming something that isn't true."

"What isn't true?"

He rubbed his smiling lips, but said nothing.

"I kept my eyes open, wide enough to see you vanish, and then he appeared. Those things couldn't happen so fast."

"Maybe, maybe not. All of this around you, Jacky boy, all of it is real." He pointed a finger at me. "Good thing you're wearing that suit."

My hand, covered in plastic, went to my chest. My

fingers spread apart and I moved them up and down. "Yeah, all the evidence is on the outside."

Pender laughed again. "Think so?"

What did he mean?

"All the evidence is on the *inside*, Jacky boy."

It hit me: hairs from my body and skin cells were on the inside; the victim's signature was on the outside. I had to destroy this suit! My fingers poked at the material covering me, trying to find an opening.

"Not going to work," Pender said.

Ignoring him, I tried to take the plastic prison off.

He crossed his arms and smiled.

I started to feel woozy. Stumbling, I fell to the floor. My eyes closed and everything around me melted away.

I woke to find myself strapped in an ordinary chair, in a small room. The transparent material that had covered my body was gone. A ball of cloth was in my mouth and my lips were smothered in duct tape. The cloth had sucked up all my saliva and my mouth felt like it was filled with sand. I barely managed to swallow and automatically breathed rapidly through my nose. My eyes traveled around the walls, but I could make out nothing except a small glass window in front of me. Pender was on the other side of the glass, in the room where I'd collapsed. The corpse was nowhere in sight.

A man entered the room and walked up to Pender. Blood suddenly rushed to my arms and face. My cheeks were burning. Who was this man? Why was he made up to appear ... *identical to me?*

Could he help me, or was he in Pender's camp? I decided to take a risk and tried to yell. The rag in my mouth muffled the cry to a quiet whimper. I twisted and wiggled, but nothing moved. I shook my head side to side. Neither of them noticed me, and I realized the pane allowed light to pass into my tiny room but not out into theirs.

I listened to them talking. My stomach squirmed. Their conversation was almost exactly the same as the one I'd had with Pender before ... before being sent to Pender's victim.

But there were differences. Pender called the man 'Jacky boy,' not 'Jack-o.' He'd always called me 'Jack-o' *before* he'd vanished, but he'd been calling me 'Jacky boy' ever since I'd finished doing ... what he'd set me up to do.

Things played out between Pender and the man almost as they had with me. Small differences, but clearly not the same.

Pender pulled the hemisphere over the man's head, clicked a few buttons, and then—

The man disappeared!

I flushed again, struggled, but I had no control.

Pender walked directly toward me. Though he couldn't see me, he smiled, lifted his arm, and waved at me.

"Hello, Jacky boy. Enjoy the show?"

I wanted to answer.

"Be a few more minutes, Jacky boy. Then we'll talk."

Not long after that, Pender came into the room, flicked the lights on, and removed my gag.

"What happened here?" I asked him.

He pulled a seat close to mine and sat, facing me. "Is it so hard to figure out?" he asked.

I thought about it, but, no, I couldn't reason it out. Unless. "Was that a recording?"

"No."

"Then what?"

"You watched me send you, Jacky boy, to another domain. Well, not you, not really. Another you."

"What other me? And what's this 'Jacky boy' business? Don't call me that. You used to call me 'Jack-o,' which was bad enough." I tried to raise my arm and swore when it would not budge. Pender patted my arm and I attempted to move away.

"I never called you 'Jack-o.' "

"You did!"

"No. Not me. Another me. The guy that called you 'Jack-o' was the one who sent you here. Me? I'm the guy you've been talking to ever since you murdered my colleague."

"What are you talking about? This place, another place, this me, another me, another you, a colleague. What … what is this all about?"

He leaned back, locking his hands behind his head.

"Let's start with you and the guy you talked to before you went to see the man you killed. Your chat with that fellow didn't happen here. That happened back where you lived until today. When you first saw my doomed friend, you were here, in this world, with me and him."

"How can that be?"

"Ever hear of the many universes?"

I shook my head.

"How about time travel?"

"Of course."

"That other guy sent you one hour into the past. It wasn't me. I sent the other you, the one that lived on this Earth, into the past. That's why you saw him disappear. He left that room," he pointed, "went to a different one. You, Jacky boy, you were sent here from another universe. The you that lived here before is gone. You are the new you that's here now. You step into his life. And you won't notice any difference. Your wife is exactly the same as when you left her."

So he wasn't planning to kill me. I asked him why not.

"Unnecessarily complicated. My buddy will never be found. Killing you would make this more complicated. Instead, you live. You go home. There'll be no questions about you. Just my ex-partner."

"What's to protect you? How do you know I won't talk about this?"

He stood and leaned toward me. "The plastic suit, Jacky boy. Any questions come up, anything happens to me, there's the plastic suit." He smirked. "You go home, enjoy your money. Forget what's happened. You'll be fine."

"Why did you kill him?" I demanded.

"I didn't. You killed him."

"Why?"

He sat back down. "He wanted half. The fool! For years he tried to find a way to send something to the future. He couldn't. Nothing worked. He didn't even try, not once, to send something to the past. 'You can't go to the past,'" he sneered. "'You could change the past if you did. But you can't change the past. So you can't go back.' Stupidity."

"So what's the answer? What did you do?"

"The obvious: I sent something to the past. It went to another Earth. No paradoxes. No problems. It didn't go to *its own past*, so it didn't *change* its past. That's how I arranged for you to commit murder."

"How?"

"All of the different versions of me in all the different universes did the same thing. I sent you to the past in some other world and swapped the different versions of you. Got you to murder that idiot."

I couldn't absorb all these ideas and asked, "How could you get all the other Penders to do what you wanted?"

Pender's eyes widened. "Good question, Jacky boy." The corners of his mouth turned down. "That's something I'm not going to tell anyone, not even you. Let's just say that all the versions of me were doing the same thing, because we're so similar, and leave it at that."

Suddenly, I wished I'd stayed at home today. "What if the me that you sent back in time hadn't showed up today? What then?"

"Ha! You," —he tapped his finger on my chest—

"you still would have come here. You would still have killed a man."

"Then there would be two of me here. What would—"

His face was hard, as if chiseled from rock. "Why do you think you're tied up?"

I would live, but only because the me that this Pender had sent back in time was now gone.

I thought of the technician who'd done my mind wipe, who'd left a sliver of my memories of darker days. Memories Pender had used.

I cursed the tech and what he'd done to me.

"Don't blame him."

"Why not? If he'd done his job properly, none of this would have happened to me."

Pender folded his arms across his chest and said, "He did his job."

"What? How can you say that? He left a piece of memory, a piece of my ... evil side."

"Yes, true, but he doesn't know that."

"What are you saying?"

"Simple, Jacky boy. He left that slice of recollection because I told him to. Amazing what people will do for a few dollars."

"You? You did this to me?"

"Why sure I did, Jacky boy. How do you think I knew to hire you for this job?"

My fingers closed into my palms.

"But don't bother the technician: he's had a tiny little mind wipe himself, and doesn't remember what he did." Pender grinned.

"You've got it all figured out, huh?"

"Yes, indeed. Don't even think of trying anything. Just go home. One more thing, Jacky boy. Aren't you curious why my dead pal wasn't able to send anything to the future?"

"No. But you're going to tell me, aren't you?"

"Someone's got to know what I've achieved. I'll wait a bit until I publish what I've found out. For now, I'll tell just you." He moved his mouth close to my ear. "You can't send anything to the future," he whispered, "because it doesn't exist yet. How utterly simple." He pulled back and shook his head. "That fool couldn't understand it. The beauty of it all is my calculations back me up."

He went on talking. I didn't pay much attention at the time, but eventually I came to wonder how serious he was about some of what he'd said. When he was done, he released me. I took my money, and this time I did snatch it from him.

Later, I realized that he'd made sure that I'd observed him sending the other me back, because he had to have someone, anyone, witness his brilliance.

He's missed one thing, plastic suit or no.

There is something I used to do, used to enjoy.

I'm coming around to thinking maybe I have one more left in me.

THE GRANDFATHER PARADOX

Having finished reading the chapter on paradoxes, he closed the book and let it slide off his leg onto the couch. He raised his right forefinger and touched the tip of his nose. His eyes rolled from side to side, then stopped as he pointed his finger upward. He agreed with the author. You can't change the past. He thought again about the grandfather paradox: if you travel back in time and kill your grandfather, then you would not be born, so you couldn't go back to kill him, so you would be born, and so on. It was a paradox only until you realized that you can't change the past.

You could go back in time, and try to kill your grandfather, but you would never succeed. There would always be something that would prevent his death, because he did not die in the past. And you can't change the past.

Perhaps the gun would jam, or you'd think you'd killed him, but he survived, or you'd killed his twin instead of him, or the physics police would stop you, or ... Or what? Suddenly, he had to find out.

He hopped up from the couch, ran toward the holding port, dashed up the ramp, and dropped into the driver's seat. After doing routine checks, flipping a switch here and there, adjusting some dials, he was ready.

The man's eyes roamed over the command console in front of him. He poked at knobs and buttons with protruding middle fingers. Sticking his tongue out of the corner of his mouth and squeezing his lips together, he pressed the *Create Wormhole* button, and a flickering appeared in front of the vessel. The saucer shaped time machine pulsated, expanding and contracting, horizontally and vertically. The required electrical energy produced jagged discharges, and the mouth of the wormhole opened. After he selected the *Stable Exotic Matter* command and chose *Hawking Method* from the menu, the craft rose and moved into the wormhole.

The time traveler soon (by his time) reached the other mouth and landed in a quiet field some distance from the house. It was well past sunset, and he could see that the party was going on, people spilling out of the house and onto the lawns, just as he expected.

He pulled his palm-com from his pocket and pressed the *Hide Time Machine* button. The saucer folded itself along the one-hundred-and-thirty-seven mutually perpendicular dimensions and disappeared from view.

He made his way past the barn, toward the house, and found his grandfather — a young man — in the back yard, alone, puffing on a pipe-full of tobacco.

"Grandfather!" he cried out.

The man turned toward him, his face wrinkled in confusion. "What did you call me? Who are you? Do I know you?"

The traveler's chest swelled. "I am your grandson. I

40

have come here in a time machine and now — get ready for this — now I am going to kill you."

The man shook his head side to side and almost laughed. "Kill me? Ha. Surely you, if you have actually traveled to your past, have heard of the — "

" — grandfather paradox. Yes, of course. Isn't this wonderful? For both of us! I will try to kill you. Something will happen to prevent you from dying, and we will find out how this will happen."

Before the man could reply, his visitor pulled out a pistol and quickly pumped two bullets into the man's heart. (The gun, of course, was silent.) Clutching his chest, eyes wide, pipe falling from his mouth, he uttered a feeble groan, and collapsed.

"You might not be dead yet." The time traveller stepped closer, took careful aim, and emptied the pistol. Ugly work, yes, but he had to know.

What would happen now? He shifted his weight from one foot to the other.

Nothing happened.

The party went on, no one came near, and nothing —

There! In the sky! A long, golden tube came down toward his grandfather. As it neared he could see it was wider than the fallen man's crumpled body.

Was this the cosmic censor? Or was it a macroscopic-sized quantum fluctuation? Or...

The cylinder continued down toward his grandfather.

No. It was aimed at him. A rose colored piece at the cylinder's end reached his feet, and moved rapidly side to side, and up. He saw that his feet were gone. His legs were gone. His torso and arms were gone.

Then the rose colored piece paused a moment. The time traveler was about to exclaim, but before he could the end of the cylinder finished its rubbing. There was a *pop-pop-popping* sound and he was all gone.

THE TEMPLATE

They came for me in the dark, in the night, in the quiet. I could see them, hear them, smell them. They had grotesquely long, skinny limbs and huge, hideous heads with slits for eyes. They never came in the light.

I called for help. "Mom! Dad!" Instead of the shout I had tried for, my words were almost silent. I called again. And again. I closed my eyes. I had to know if it had worked. When I looked they were still there. More inaudible cries. Somehow, my mother knew and came to my bedroom.

She raised her hand to her mouth as she stared at them, and asked, "What are they?"

My father, a step behind her, said, "What's the matter? What are you looking at?"

We pointed, but he never saw them. When he flipped on the lights, the demons were gone.

"Mom, did you see them? Please don't let them come anymore."

Her face went blank. "What do you mean, Ben? What did you see?"

I told her, and my father.

Mom inevitably replied, "Dear, everything is all right. It was only your imagination." She'd pick me up and hug me, cooing to me, whispering that it had just been a bad dream, that it was all in my head.

I endured this almost every night.

My parents tried to convince me that these were just nightmares. The monsters were not real. I knew better.

They took me to one psychiatrist after another. The shrinks convinced me that the creatures were only in my mind. By the time I was a young man I was in agreement that these were my imaginings.

It wasn't until I was a professor that I began again to question what was real and what was not. It was through my research in physics that I came to wonder again about the nature of reality. I chose to study what was, at that time, a respectable research topic: theoretical time travel. I often wish I could go back to that, but the experiments have made this impossible.

Kitt Bell and I were, unofficially, the leaders of the two opposing theoretical views of time travel. Kitt's group believed that backward time travel was impossible. My colleagues said it could be done.

Kitt and I had met long before, when we were both early in our careers as physics professors. We were at the thirtieth annual conference for research on studies of the arrow of time, investigating why time only goes forward. Kitt and I had given presentations regarding theoretical time travel. I remember finishing mine, answering some questions, and returning to my front row seat for Kitt's talk.

I watched her as she walked to the front of the lecture room. Her strides were graceful. She had short, blond, curly hair. Dressed in a white, long-sleeved top, a light blue vest, and deep blue slacks, Kitt set up her laptop. I realized she had asked me a question after my talk—I could not recall what it was—and I had been able to answer it only because her seat was well back in the room. Had she been this close to me when she'd asked her question, I would have been as I was now, sitting so near to her. She was smiling at me as I looked into her eyes. There was a brightness about her. She was well into her presentation before I knew she had started, and I was hopelessly lost. I tried to pick up some of what she was saying.

Her talk was the last for that session, so after she'd answered questions I moved quickly toward her.

"Your work is very interesting," I said, scratching my neck. What next? If only I could remember something of her presentation. "I am intrigued by your analysis of what you called the unstable, closed, time-like loops. Would you have time for coffee, to talk more about this, or," I glanced at my watch, "perhaps dinner or a drink?"

Her eyes twinkled. She touched her lower lip with a finger and said, "Only if you'll tell me more about your multiple universes."

Then she smiled at me again. Moments later, we had decided on drinks and dinner.

"So you believe, Ben Artemit, that it is possible to send physical matter, or perhaps light, to the past?" she asked. Her drinking glass vibrated rhythmically as she strummed it with her fingernails.

"Indeed I do."

"But you don't believe you can change the past?" she said.

"Correct. Because—"

"—whatever you send to the past leaves our universe and goes to a different one."

"Which cannot affect *our* past," I finished.

She sipped her drink, set it down, and leaned forward. "How do you propose to prove your theory?" she asked, tapping her finger on the table between us.

"I have a way," I said, scratching my cheek.

"Do you?" She smiled mischievously. "What is it?"

I told her. She nodded and asked, "How do you get that idea across to your undergraduate students?"

I set my drink down, raised my forefinger, and pulled two articles out of my bag.

"What do you have there?"

I held them up. "This is, as you know, a piece of paper, and this," I rolled the instrument between my fingers, "is a pen."

Her eyes darted between the pen and paper. "What are you doing with those?"

"This is what people used, long ago, as recently as the 2090s, to write, and calculate."

"I know what they are, but why do you have those antiques?"

"I do some of my calculations using pen and paper."

"Why?"

"The symbols are made by *me*, not by some computer. They grow into richer and fuller forms. *I* make them grow." I was beaming.

"And when you're done?"

I was about to answer when she continued, her eyes closing and opening slowly.

"You scan them into your computer and then re-move the ink from the paper, so you can use the paper over and over."

"Yes. I get more ink as I need it."

She traced a finger across the paper. "Show me. Use your pen."

I placed the paper between us and drew a line on the page, and an arrow pointing up the line. At the top I wrote '2 p.m.' and at the bottom I wrote '1 p.m.' Then I drew a dashed semicircle that went from the '2 p.m.' to the '1 p.m.' and a downward arrow on this curve.

"Wait," said Kitt. She reached for the pen, took it from my hand, her fingers touching mine. She tried to write with the pen, but she was not holding it prop-erly. She lifted the pen from the paper, tilted her head to the side, and laughed. Then she returned the pen to my hand.

I breathed in the apple scent of her hair. My fingers were on the verge of shaking. I concentrated.

"Please go on," she encouraged. "Continue with your drawing, what you tell your students."

"Suppose we have a machine that can send a mes-sage to the past, from 2 p.m. to 1 p.m.," I began. "We make the machine send a signal to itself, but at the earlier time. That's what I'm indicating here by this dashed curve. Let's have this machine hooked up to a computer. We tell the computer *not* to send a signal out, at 2 p.m., if it *does* receive the signal at 1 p.m. We also instruct the computer to send out the message at 2 p.m. if it receives nothing at 1 p.m. Therefore, if a message arrives at 1 p.m., nothing is sent out at 2 p.m."

"Right," she said. "The paradox: where did the signal come from?"

"Exactly," I said, and finished my drink. "My answer is: it came from another universe. From one of the infinitely many universes in the many worlds interpretation of quantum mechanics."

"The signal is sent out, at 2 p.m., from people in a universe where they did *not* receive one at 1 p.m."

"And this signal is received in another universe," I added.

"So, in one of the universes, a message is sent at 2 p.m. and nothing is received at 1 p.m., while in the other universe, a signal is received at 1 p.m. and nothing goes out at 2 p.m." She paused. "Does this work well with the students? I mean, if you go slowly through it?"

"Quite nicely, yes."

"Do you tell them about the splitting of the universe?"

"Yes," I replied. "I say that the instant the signal is to be received, the universe splits into two."

"One where the signal *is* received and one where it is *not*."

I smiled. "These are the two universes we have been talking about."

Kitt leaned back in her chair, but suddenly sat up. "None of this is possible."

"I know. Your theory says it can't be done."

"Right."

"Let's talk more," I suggested.

Later, as I reflected on the complicated mathematical details in our different theories, I was glad that humans had no technology to test them, to perform experiments that would show which was correct and which was wrong. I didn't know then that Kitt and I would actually see the predictions of our theories being scrutinized.

While Kitt and I disagreed about time travel to the past, we agreed on many fundamental issues. Perhaps most important was that an observation could be considered to have been made only if it had been done by a conscious observer. We both took this consciousness interpretation seriously. As I think back on it all, neither of us took it seriously enough. That we had not thought sufficiently about this would change both of our lives, and would have an impact that neither of us would ever have thought possible.

The difference is that Kitt doesn't know this, and I do.

Our theories were only a matter of debate until Al Turen proposed a way of actually sending a message to the past. "After all," he said to us, his hand on his hip and his finger wagging in the air, "we know this is going to make history. We are going to find out, *really find out*, whether or not you can go back in time, or at least send a message back in time." His head bobbed up and down as if it sat on a spring.

Turen's breakthrough led to the historic experiments and, in turn, to the ultimate publication that gave the experimental observations and presented the theoretical view that ended the debate. The results showed that time travel to the past cannot happen. What is done is done and cannot be undone. You can`t go back.

Even though you can. Kitt Bell, Al Turen, and I had proven that you *can* travel back in time. The predicament I was in was that I *remembered* that we had witnessed backward time travel, but Kitt and Turen didn't.

My one direct experience with the dark side of Turen showed me what he was capable of. He had a student, Sally Burton, who later became my student. She hadn't received permission to work on the theoretical problem that so fascinated her. Her supervisor, Al Turen, didn't do theoretical work, although he knew enough to be able to read it and understand some of it.

Sally later told me that she had done the calculation, even though Turen had told her not to, because she found the attraction too great to resist. Sally worked secretly on her special project. She pushed the work along, believing that Turen would be so impressed that he would allow her analysis for her dissertation. She was only fifteen at the time.

One morning after she had solved the problem, she

had gone in to the university and waited until her supervisor arrived.

I usually did not reach the university early in the morning, but that day was an exception. I had a meeting to attend. I was just coming through the doorway a bit down the hall from Turen's office when I heard Sally speak.

"Professor Turen?" she said, in a small voice. I remember that Sally had the popular rainbow hairdo: her hair went from red at her forehead, through all the colors, ending with blue and indigo at the back of her neck.

"Sally?" Turen queried.

I stopped walking, breathed quietly.

She stepped into his office, leaving the door open enough that I could see her and Turen. I stood as still as possible.

"What is it?" he asked her.

"I have solved the problem. I have finished it. Here, I wrote a summary for you." She handed it to him.

I heard him grumbling and muttering.

"I told you not to work on this!" he suddenly yelled, his arms flying through the air.

"But I have —"

"You have wasted your time! Do you want to get your Ph.D. or not? Keep this up and you are finished." He tossed the material she had given him into the garbage. "Out!" he screamed, as he stood up and pointed to the doorway. She moved away from him, but he moved closer, until their noses were almost touching. They were both five feet in height. "Do the work I assigned you. Or quit." She backed out of his office and he slammed the door shut.

I heard her crying, as she ran away from his office and out of the building. That was the last I saw of her until three years ago. She left the university, and didn't come back until enough time had gone by for her to heal. When she did return, she became my student, and went on to do outstanding research.

In the meantime, Al Turen had published the work she had done. He hadn't included her name on the paper, hadn't even mentioned her in his acknowledgements. From what others have told me, he's done much worse.

When Turen announced he had a way to send a message to the past, he claimed that he wanted the first experiments to be done with Kitt and me present.

We agreed that the three of us would meet and watch the experiments being done. We would do the self-consistent mode—where a signal is sent out only if a signal is received, and no signal goes out if none comes in—and the paradox mode, the way Kitt and I had discussed when we first met. First, we would do the experiments manually, so we could see for ourselves what would happen. Turen had set things up so that we would see a big, red flash if the photon stream—the signal—was detected. After we'd done enough observations, automation would be set up to do a large number of trials and compare them against the two theoretical models: Kitt's life's work and mine.

I preferred the paradox set-up because just one experiment with the arrival of a signal and no signal sent

could be understood only by my many worlds interpretation. It would counter Kitt's claim that backward
time travel was impossible.

Kitt, of course, wanted to start with the self-consistent set-up: she wanted to see all experiments showing
no signal in and *no signal out*.

I knew Kitt well enough to know that she didn't
just *want*, but actually *needed*, to have her theory shown
to be true. The paradox set-up could wipe out her life's
work with just one experiment, and hurt her more
deeply than she ever had been before. I was thankful
that Turen did not know this about Kitt.

On the day of the experiments, Kitt couldn't eat
and couldn't sleep. I understood. What would I do if
my lifetime achievements were suddenly obliterated
by experiments?

Turen didn't care whether we started with the paradox or self-consistent experiments: we would do both
anyway, and he just needed to get experimental observations that would establish whether or not time travel
was possible. As a bonus, he would get to see one of
us fail.

The three of us came together in Turen's lab to perform the experiments that would settle the issue. He
tossed a coin to choose which experiments we would
start with, and announced that we would begin with
the paradox set-up.

We agreed not to tamper with the apparatus between the earlier time of detecting the signal — a stream
of photons — and the later time of sending it out. We
readied ourselves to watch what would happen.

On the first attempt, there was a bright flash of red. The stream of photons had arrived at the detector before the signal was to have been sent into the past! Despite my awareness of how very much this would bother Kitt, I was ... relieved.

Without thinking, I walked up to, and focused on, the red bulb. With Kitt and Turen behind me, I said, "We will now see that no signal will be sent, not by us. This means the message has come from another world, another universe. In that other world, the three of us, so to speak, did not receive the stream of photons, and so they will send a signal, and that signal is the one that we all just observed."

Then I heard Kitt say, "No!" I looked back and saw that her hand covered her mouth. She'd turned so that Turen was behind her. Kitt's eyes glistened but she blinked back the tears. She lowered her hand—it was shaking, barely perceptibly—and said, "This can't be happening. It's not possible. It doesn't ... make sense..."

"It does," I said, quietly.

The words had spilled out of me too quickly. I'd been too focused on *my* theory, *my* work. Now I had to deal with the consequences. I forced myself to look at Kitt again.

She was taking deep, slow breaths. She cleared her throat quietly and smoothed her shirt with her hand. Her eyes drifted from the walls to the floor.

My forehead and cheeks prickled from needles of heat. I started to walk toward her, my hand rising to touch her. But Turen was speaking. My window had closed.

"Ten seconds until we see whether or not the signal will be sent," he said.

"It won't be sent," I whispered.

Kitt was silent.

We all waited.

The instant arrived.

No signal was sent.

It bothers me to admit it, but, in spite of myself, and what I had just done, I think I might have smiled. "We received the signal," I heard myself saying, "and no signal was sent. So it must have come from a group like us ... doing the same work ... in their own world."

Turen's grin grew, and grew. He looked over at Kitt and, with his hand on his hip and his finger wobbling in her face, said, "That pretty much settles things, don't you agree, Kitt?"

This was too much for me to accept. Enough was enough. I knew all too well that he took pleasure in others' failures. Except for Sally, I'd convinced myself that there was nothing I could do, and that it was all right to leave these people to deal with their problems by themselves. But this was a cheap shot at Kitt. I wasn't going to stand by and watch as he aimed at her.

Suddenly, and inexplicably, I'd wanted it to be possible for *both* Kitt and me to be right. Before I'd realized the hopelessness of this desire, everything had changed. Turen had lost his grin. The mood had lightened in some way. I'd sensed that somehow everything had been suspended, that nothing had been decided.

Kitt was no longer upset. She seemed to be puzzled more than anything else. She simply ignored Turen, looked at me instead, and in a very soft voice said, "I don't understand, Ben. Why do you say we received a signal? We did not. We all saw that ... there was no red flash. No signal arrived. That is why one was just sent out."

I looked at her and the muscles in my face tightened. What was going on? Why had Kitt just said that no signal had come in, and that one had just gone out? Exactly the opposite was what had really happened! I ran my tongue between my lips and shook my head. I said, "Kitt, didn't you see the red flash? We *did see* the signal arrive. Just a moment ago. That's why no signal was sent." I turned to Turen in a silent appeal, hoping he would explain to Kitt what we had just seen.

He had a deep frown and his face was red. He said to me, speaking quickly and forcefully, "What are you talking about, Artemit? You saw a red flash? I didn't see a flash! No signal was received. That is why the apparatus sent one out, sent it to the so-called time machine." He took a deep breath and said, this time one word at a time, "No signal arrived. So a signal was sent."

What was happening here? We'd — or at least I'd — seen the evidence, and it confirmed my theory. Why were Kitt and Turen denying it? "We did detect the signal," I insisted. "Just look at the recording."

Turen showed it to us.

It revealed that ... no signal had been received!

I had just seen that a signal had been received, and

now Kitt and Turen, and the computer, were all telling me that what I had seen was not what they had seen.

Then it hit me, and hard. My demons were back. The hideous, grotesque creatures were back in my mind. I *had* seen them and remembered them, though no one else had. In that moment I knew, *I knew* that those horrible beings were real, as real as the arrival of the photon stream. There was no doubt for me. I knew now what I had known as a boy, all those years ago, that only *I* could see what was really happening. The world was as *I* saw it and, for some reason, others were seeing something different. My mother hadn't remembered the monsters, my father hadn't even seen them, and now Kitt and Turen didn't remember what I did.

I couldn't allow them to know what I'd seen. I had to play along. Kitt and Turen agreed; I could see that.

Kitt said, "No signal was received." She looked at Turen.

He nodded and said, "Nothing was detected. That is why the apparatus then sent out a signal."

As bad as things were, they got worse. Kitt was now shaking her head. She frowned, swallowed, and looked at Turen. She said, her voice steady and firm, "What are you saying, Al? We did not send a signal. We observed no signal in and we sent none out. It all makes sense. Think about it. No signal in, no signal out. The apparatus was designed that way."

"*What?*" I whispered. I covered my head with my hands, was still for a moment, and then scratched the top of my head. Now Kitt was saying no signal had been sent. A moment ago she had said that one *had* been sent! Now Kitt and Turen were disagreeing! It wasn't just me. They had separate realities. They remembered differently.

Turen then said, almost in a growl, "We didn't set up in the self-consistent mode Kitt, we're in the paradox mode: the apparatus is set up to send a signal if it does not receive one."

Kitt interjected, "Let's look at the recording. Show it to us, Al."

He did.

A signal had been sent.

"So why are you saying nothing went out?" he asked Kitt.

She replied, "I never said that. Of course a signal was sent. No signal arrived, so a signal was sent."

A moment passed in silence. Kitt seemed satisfied. Turen just waited.

I had no idea what to do or what to say. It required a huge effort to keep myself from trembling. I don't know how I managed it. Reality wasn't something independent of us, although I don't think I thought about that just then. Kitt and Turen and I were creating reality. No, not just creating it, changing it as well.

The final record said that no signal had come in and that one had subsequently been sent out. That was also what Kitt and Turen ended up remembering.

But not me. I knew what had really happened, just as I had known what really happened when I was a boy. I now realized that I would have horrible experiences ahead of me. My life had just changed.

We continued on, doing more experiments.

I knew that the second time was going to be the same, and it was. We all saw the red flash. I then said that no signal would be sent. Kitt was lost in disbelief. The time for emitting the photon stream came, and no signal was sent. Then Kitt said that no signal had arrived. Turen agreed. I asked to check the recording. No signal had been detected. Kitt explained that this was because we were using the self-consistent mode. No signal arrived, no signal was sent, she said. Still, Turen remembered a signal had been sent. The recording was checked and a signal had indeed gone out. They agreed that no signal had been detected, and that later one was sent out.

Over and over again, backward time travel was found to occur. Kitt and Turen remembered that it had never been seen, not even once, and the computer confirmed this as well.

I withdrew as more experiments were done, and they argued some more, until they both remembered the same thing, and until the recording was what they ended up remembering. With each experiment, their arguing dwindled, until it all became routine.

After we had done several experiments, the task of carrying out a large number of experiments was turned over to the automation.

They wrote up what they had seen and reported that backward time travel was never experimentally observed. Their paper appeared on-line within hours.

Later, the experiments were repeated by others. They followed the procedure specified in the paper and found the same results.

Backward time travel was unequivocally demonstrated many times in our experiments, and I believe the same may have happened with other groups of investigators.

Of course, everyone agreed that backward time travel had never happened.

That's what everybody remembered, and that's what ended up being recorded.

You can't travel to the past. What is done is done and can't be undone. You can't go back.

Even though you can.

Later, after all the experiments had been analyzed, I realized that a template had been formed. Initially, what that template would be was not clear. We had done a quantum experiment, in which we might or might not find backward time travel to occur. For a while, as we debated, what the result would be was not established. In the end, I was alone in remembering time travel to the past. Kitt and Turen, and then all the others, had selected a different answer, had shown time travel to the past to be impossible.

In the dynamics of our interactions, the template was created. Once formed, it was indelible. The same results were seen repeatedly because the template made it so.

The template had started to form when I had wished that both Kitt and I would be right. The experiments had confirmed Kitt's theory, negated mine. Although I was the only one who remembered, my theory had also been proven: signals had been sent to the past.

This was just the time travel template.

I wonder now about all the other templates. I wonder which have been formed, and which are still in the process of forming. Worst of all, I wonder about my childhood monsters and what might be in store for me now.

PROLONGING THE INEVITABLE

One of us was going to get hurt, and badly. It would be either my colleague, Kitt Bell, or me, Ben Artemit. If it were Kitt, she would be forced to accept that her life's work, her greatest achievement, was wrong. That, in itself, would devastate her. But to find this out after she had witnessed, time and time again, experiments that had proven her work to be fully correct, would harm her beyond description. Kitt could be spared this pain if I faced a horror that is almost unbelievable: I would have to confront my childhood monsters. One of us would be saved, but the other would be destroyed.

It would be up to me to choose.

When I was a boy, they would come for me every night. They were hideous, frightening creatures. They had skinny, long, dark limbs that glistened like slime. Their heads were bloated, impossibly huge. It was only I who saw and remembered them. My mother saw them, but my father didn't, and my mom didn't remember seeing them. My parents and their squad of shrinks eventually convinced me that these uninvited visitors were all in my mind.

I was the only person who saw and remembered the actual experimental results, and had to face everyone remembering differently than I did. I only began to understand when we did the time travel experiments.

The monsters were real. They would come back. Who were they? What did they want? Would they harm me? Could I somehow avoid them?

I asked myself these questions for two full days after the experiments. Kitt celebrated when she learned that the scientific community had verified her theory. Turen enjoyed having settled the issue by experiments. I withdrew.

Knowing that the monsters would return left me shaking uncontrollably, and I had no idea what to do. When I was a boy they came for me only in the dark, only when I was sent to bed, to go to sleep. So, in these two full days and three full nights, I refused to sleep. I kept all the lights on and racked my brain for a way out of this mess.

The only idea that made any sense was for me to talk with the one and only friend I had. If my friend would listen to me, help me think, then maybe I could block the horror.

But I couldn't, for my one and only friend in the solar system was none other than Kitt. If I told her that these demons awaited me and told her what had really happened, both with the time travel experiments and my experiences as a youth, Kitt might actually believe me. If she did, then she would lose her great, lifetime achievement. I couldn't bear to see this happen to her.

More likely, Kitt would not believe me. I would have to face the creatures alone and live with the knowledge that Kitt would think less of me. I couldn't face that either. I simply could not tell her.

It had been three nights now that I had not had the courage to sleep. I had no new ideas and I was running out of time.

It was time to act, but I had no idea what to do. I'd made no progress indoors, so I decided to go for a walk. Maybe I'd get an idea. I opened the door —

— and Kitt was standing right there. I congratulated her on her success. She thanked me. Kitt's blue eyes blinked quickly a couple of times. Placing a finger on her lower lip, she said, "Please don't take this the wrong way, Ben, but you look terrible. Have you even slept these last two days?"

No doubt, my appearance left nothing to question. "No, Kitt, I haven't."

"You must be very sad about the experiments," she said.

I simply nodded.

"It's more than that though," she said.

I was silent.

"Well? Are you going to tell me about it, or not?"

I suggested that we walk a bit, maybe stop for coffee. What would I say to her? I decided to tell some of the truth, but not all. We got our coffee and took a table in the far corner, away from other customers.

Kitt waited, looked at me, tapping her forefinger rapidly on the tabletop. "You cannot do this, Ben! You simply cannot raise a subject like this and then clamp down. No. Not acceptable."

She'd finished. We both knew she had me, and now

I would have to tell her something. I looked into my coffee and scratched the top of my head. Then I said, "OK. I'll tell you." I paused. What to say? Where to start? "Suppose, just suppose—and I'm not admitting to anything, at least not yet—suppose that I told you I noticed something odd about the experiments, but nobody else did. I tried to tell you, and Turen, and ... neither of you agreed with me. Neither of you remembered what I'd noticed. What would you say to that?"

She tilted her head to one side and said, "Well, what did you see? Why wouldn't we pay attention to it?"

"Before we go there Kitt, please: just suppose that this happened, just as I've described it. What would you think about that, about me? Honestly."

"Of course I'll be honest," she protested. And then she finally said it. "I'd think that something happened ... to you ... because why wouldn't anyone else notice? I mean, especially if it's as important as you think it is."

"So, basically, you're saying, kindly, that you'd think I'd lost it, that I was crazy? Right?"

Kitt shifted in her chair. "OK. Yes. Something like that."

"So you see my problem!" I chopped the air with my right hand. "If I tell you what actually happened, you'll think I'm nuts."

I had put myself in an awkward situation, but having Kitt near me, just talking with her was helping. I had no idea, at that point in our conversation, just how far this was going to take Kitt into the strange and disturbing world I knew all too well. If I'd known what was in store for her I wouldn't have said another word.

She looked at me, with a hint of a smile on her lips. "What if I promise not to think you're crazy? Would you tell me what you saw? Could you tell me why it's so important?" Her eyes widened and she quickly added, "I don't mean your work isn't important. It is. I—"

"No, Kitt: my work is not important." I shook my head, wrapped my hands around my cup, and put my arms down on the table. "Not anymore. Not to me. I've lost that. That's not what's wrong. That's what I'm trying to tell you. What is wrong, what I'm up against, is so much worse than me losing my theory…"

Kitt reached over the table and put her hand on my arm. Then she spoke quietly, but intensely. "Whatever this is, you've got to trust me. You've opened up to me because you think I can help. So tell me what it is."

"If I tell you, and you believe me, you are going to lose your life's work. And if you don't believe me…"

Kitt moved her hand from my arm and gently drummed her fingers on the tabletop. Her eyes scanned the room, and then fixed on me. "Ben, I cannot lose my life's work, no matter what is troubling you. I saw the experiments and I know my work is sound, and I won't lose that. So, tell me what this is all about."

My fear of those creatures won out, made me choose to ask for Kitt's help. Knowing deep down that I was risking Kitt's happiness, I told her everything.

"Kitt, I know that you're probably going to think that I'm imagining all of this, that it's all in my mind." I hung my head, looked down at my coffee cup, and exhaled deeply, realizing only then that I'd been holding my breath.

"Go on, I'm listening," she said.

"It's not about my theory, not anymore. I had to tell you about the experiments because if you find that hard to accept, what I'm going to tell you now is ... it's going to sound ludicrous. What happened to me when we did the experiments made me realize that the monsters my mother and I saw, but only I remembered, *really did exist*. Just like those experiments! And now I ... I'm afraid," I whispered, "I'm afraid they are going to come back."

When I heard Kitt's next comment, I thought that she hadn't heard what I'd whispered.

"Wait, Ben. I want to talk more about the experiments. Why don't we just go and do them again? If what you say is true, I want to see it for myself. Can we prove what you've said? Why can't we go back and do them again and this time get—I don't know how—get an indisputable record of the results? Hard evidence that will prove what you're saying?"

"No, Kitt!" I swept my hand in front of me, and almost stood up. "No. I don't want to do any more experiments. I saw what you went through before, and I don't want to see you go through that again. Trust me. It's not the experiments that bother me. It's what happened to me when I was a boy. There's no point doing the experiments again because we'll just get the same results."

She leaned toward me. "It's up to me to decide what I want! I want to see what you've seen. How can you say we'll just get the same results?"

I started to tell her why, but she interrupted.

"If you were in my position right now, what would you do? Could you just accept my saying so? Wouldn't you want to see for yourself?"

She had me again. I couldn't argue, and I regretted having gotten myself into this position. Still I wasn't going to give up, not just yet. "There's no point Kitt. In the end, just like before, you won't remember, and we can't make a permanent record: the final record in the computer was the same as what both you and Turen remembered, and it's not going to be any different now."

"If I'm just going to remember the same as I did before, what harm can that do me? OK, sure, if I go through what you saw before, that will bother me, but only until it's all over, and then I'll feel just the same as I do now. So in the end I'm not going to be harmed."

"But Kitt, it devastated you, and — "

"It might devastate me again, but I feel just fine right now. Besides, we can make a permanent record."

I raised my eyebrows. I asked, "How can we possibly do that?"

"Let's suppose it all happened just as you say it did. We did the experiments. We argued. In the end we got our way and you lost out. There were two of us remembering one thing, and just you remembering another thing. Let's go back, just you and me Ben, and do it all over again."

"How can I explain this?" I sighed. "What we saw before, what ended up as your memory, and what the computer recorded: that result has been selected, out of all possible outcomes, as the final and definitive result." I shrugged. "We won't see anything different Kitt."

"Maybe not. So here's what we do. One: we do different experiments. Two: we won't use the computer to make a record."

I scratched my head. "What experiments will we do this time?"

"We will program the computer to send a signal to five minutes in the past, but only if it *did not* receive a signal five minutes ago, and we tell the computer *not* to send a signal if it *did* receive one."

I opened my hands and said, "But that's just what we did last time."

"I know. This time, if we receive a signal, we will *change the computer program*, and have it send out a *different* signal than the one received. If this happens, the *only* possible explanation is that the signal received —"

" —was sent from a different universe," I concluded.

Our pass codes were still active, and we had no trouble getting into Turen's lab. It was, as we expected, deserted: Turen would still be celebrating, no doubt about that.

We had to wipe the computer's record of the results, but still record them in some fashion that would convince her as to what we actually observed, before any discussion, before her memory could be changed. How could we do that?

We would *write* the results as they occurred, using a very old method, dating back to the 2090s: we would write them using pens. On the way to the lab we had picked up two pens and two pieces of paper from my place. We agreed that Kitt would record positive time travel results — signals having traveled back in time — and I would record negative or 'null' results: no evidence of backward time travel. The pattern of the letters and words you write by hand is unique: my 'handwriting' and Kitt's were easily distinguished. We agreed to make these records as soon as they occurred, before we discussed them or argued. For example, for a signal coming in and a different signal going out, Kitt would write: 'SI-DSO (KB).' If no signal came in, I would write: 'NSI (BA).'

On our first two trials, no signal arrived.

On our third trial, we received a signal.

"No!" Kitt covered her nose and mouth with her hands. She stared at me. She did not move at all. Then she began to quiver and the sobs broke through. This is how she must have felt before, but last time, she held it inside, because Turen was present. Now, her eyes asked me to find a way to change this result.

I wanted somehow to soothe her pain. "Kitt, I—"

She broke in. "Oh, Ben! All that you told me is true!" She was crying openly now. "Ben, *I remember!* I remember all those experiments we did. They went just as you said. A signal arrived ... I was upset ... We argued ... Oh, no. I remember it all. And now it's happening again. A signal has arrived. This means ... my work ... all of it..." she sniffled, "wrong."

I shouldn't have agreed to do these experiments.

What if Kitt remembered this time, and lost what she had? I wanted Kitt to have back what she had before.

While I was thinking this, scientist that she was, Kitt had written down 'SR (KB).' The pen fell from her hand. I wished she could have it all back, that her recollection of these experiments that we were now doing could, somehow, preserve her theory, and her life's work. I remember, as clearly as if this had happened yesterday. I wanted this for Kitt, and I wanted it very much.

That is when it all happened. It was as if time had stopped, and everything had been changed: this was all around me, and also inside me. It was as if a loud, booming, pounding noise had suddenly stopped and been replaced by an absolute, roaring silence.

I looked at Kitt and I knew then that ... it had happened again! Just like before, when we'd done the experiments the first time.

All around me, things had changed. Subtly, but unequivocally.

I watched Kitt.

A moment passed.

"Three in a row: no signal in," she said.

I could not believe the change I saw in her. A moment ago, she had tears streaming down her cheeks and she had been sobbing. Now she was totally relaxed. There was no sign that she'd been upset.

In a blur, I grabbed my paper and pen and recorded: 'NSI (BA).' Just as quickly, I realized it might be hopeless: Kitt's paper would still have her handwritten record that a signal had been received. I picked up her piece of paper. It was blank! What she had written was no longer there. Just as when we'd done the experiments before, the record had changed.

Could we actually get out of this without Kitt losing her success? Kitt would not agree to stop after three experiments, so I couldn't suggest that we quit. We had to go on, or she would be suspicious of the results. I made sure we continued and set things up to do another experiment.

Suddenly, and with no build-up or warning whatsoever, every single molecule in my body tingled. I knew, even before I turned to look. I knew they were there. Watching me. Analyzing me. Planning. I don't know where the courage came from, but I willed myself to turn. To look back at them. I saw two creatures. The hideous grins. The large heads and slit-like eyes. I sensed evil. One of them raised an upper limb so its joint was above its head, and pointed at me. My entire body trembled, yet I could do nothing.

Then they disappeared.

Kitt was incredulous.

"What ... what happened to you Ben?" Her mouth hung open and her face was blank. "What's happened?" she asked again.

I wanted to tell her, but I needed to get out of this place. "I'll explain later. Let's just finish the experiments and leave."

Every time a signal was received, we both suffered through the result. The only difference between us was that, each time, her memory changed. I was grateful that Kitt would remember none of this.

Eventually, mercifully, we had gone through only three results with a signal received and a different signal sent, and also eight results with no signal received. Kitt didn't remember the three signals received: her recollection was that these too had been cases where no signal had come in. As a result, I had recorded, in my handwriting, that we had witnessed eleven experiments confirming her theory. With these eleven results, I convinced Kitt that we had done enough. None of what Kitt had written remained on the paper she had used. Once again, the record of the experiments had been changed.

"OK, Kitt," I said as I passed my piece of paper to her, "all null results."

She looked at her piece of paper, and my piece of paper, and nodded. Her eyes met mine. "What do you think this means?"

"I think it means that there is no backward time travel." I took a deep breath, turned away, and began to pace. "There was, for me, in our experiments three days ago, time travel. That's all over with now, for all of us, including me. There can no longer be backward time travel, the sending of signals into the past," I lied. "Not for me, or for any of us — not in our universe, anyway."

"But there was, before, for you Ben. You witnessed signals being sent back, didn't you?"

"Yes. I did. I truly did. I know it sounds strange..."

"Quantum physics is strange," Kitt agreed. Looking into my eyes, she said, "I believe you Ben. I don't know why … but I do. I wasn't sure before, not really, but I am now."

I had to get out of the lab. We left and started to walk to my home. My mind was off of time travel and fully back onto the demons awaiting me. I needed Kitt's help, but I didn't want to ask for it. I wouldn't ask for it.

Kitt stopped walking and so did I. I sensed that she had not forgotten everything.

"What happened back there Ben? What was it? You were frightened, weren't you?"

I was thinking about how I could answer her when she spoke again.

"While we were having coffee, you told me about the monsters you saw in the dark when you were a child. You said that you were frightened then, and afraid again today."

I didn't want to tell Kitt, but knew I needed to confide in her. Reluctantly, I described the brief instant where I had seen them, staring and grinning in the lab just a short time ago. At that moment, I realized *it was not dark.*

I don't know what Kitt thought, but I wanted her to stay with me.

As if reading my mind she asked, "What do we do now? You need to sleep Ben, and you shouldn't be alone."

I nodded.

"Let's go back. You won't be alone."

That meant more to me than I can explain. Kitt

knew that my fears were real, at least to me. I would now have to face my fears.

I was too worried just then to realize the implications of these experiments, but I did later. My reality allowed for the sending of signals back in time. More than that, I also had some kind of power. It was somehow due to me that Kitt had been able to see the experiments with backward time travel, and that it was somehow because of me that Kitt had actually remembered what had occurred in the very first experiments, even though she'd ended up forgetting. I had some sort of ability to choose what would happen, an ability that I didn't want to have. If I could change Kitt's reality, I could change the realities of others too, and I was not comfortable with this kind of power. It would be some time before I would understand that I had changed Kitt's handwritten record, an ability that I might need when the time came to face the demons.

As we walked, it seemed to me that some good had come out of this. We had done the experiments that had satisfied Kitt, and her reality had been preserved. Her theory and her happiness were safe. We had used Al Turen's lab, and left it just as we'd found it. He would never know we had been there.

It seems incredible to me now that I had thought such things. I was wrong about so much. Al Turen had, of course, recorded everything we had done, and I cannot explain why I didn't realize that then.

I was right about one thing. Turen was not the only one to see all that had happened, and I would soon find out more.

75

I shuddered to think of what was just ahead of me. I had to live in my reality and face my childhood monsters.

They had been watching and were ready now. I knew they would come for me this night.

COME THE CHILDHOOD MONSTERS

^^^

In their dark world, the two twisted, hideous, thin-limbed forms plotted and planned.

"Does he know?" asked one.

A pause, then the other said, "No. We can see no way that he could. We are almost certain he does not know."

The first one hissed, its upper limbs thrashing. "'Almost?' You say 'almost?' That's not good enough. We need to be certain. Need I remind you what is at stake?"

"I know what is at stake!" the other said, its eye-slits opening and closing spasmodically. "We all know ... We have been working on this relentlessly, and we do not see what more could be done. And ... we must act."

The first one brought its limbs to its sides and stopped moving them. "So be it. We have re-established the link?"

"Yes! Yes. This we are certain of!" Its eye-slits opened wide and it raised the end of one upper limb to its mouth. "We have found him actively involved in the quantum experiments, and this has led us back to him."

"Can he do it?"

"We think so. But we must persuade him."

"And if you do not convince him?"

"We must. That gives us our best chance."

"If you do not convince him, then what will you tell him?" The first one stroked its upper limbs together.

The other's eye-slits closed as it whispered, "That we will remove his brain, and do our best to use it to get what we need."

* * *

Without so much as a knock at the door, or even taking the time to see if the door was locked, Al Turen burst into my home and started in on Kitt and me. Only five feet tall, Turen nevertheless managed to fill the doorway, his arms stiff at his sides, his chest rising and falling. Kitt automatically took a step back and partly behind me, placing her hand on my shoulder. I scratched my head but gave him no other reaction.

"How dare you two! Who do you think you are? You are just a couple of theorists." He stomped his foot. "Without me you'd have nothing. You break into my lab and use it without even ... without me!"

On and on he went, until he finally ran out of adrenaline. We had just come back from doing experiments in his lab, and hadn't realized until now that, of course, he would record anything and everything going on in his lab.

"Granted, we were wrong to do that," said Kitt, pressing her fingers into my shoulder. "We just had to know for sure."

"I have it all recorded. I watched everything you two did. Look!" His face was red enough to start a fire and one of the veins at his temple pulsed noticeably.

Turen called up his computer and played the holo for us, without giving us a chance to say anything. I didn't want to face the replay. Kitt didn't remember what had happened, not everything. I did. I squirmed as I thought about what the holo would reveal.

It showed the two of us doing the time travel experiments. The recording had begun with our entrance into the lab. I held my breath as I watched. Would we see what Kitt remembered, that her theory had been confirmed as true? I very much wanted that. Or, would it show what had actually happened, that some of the experiments verified my theory, showed that time travel to the past had happened, and thus proved Kitt's theory to be wrong? I craved for someone other than myself to see what I'd seen. I had another reason for desiring this outcome: I knew that my childhood monsters, real and grotesque beings, were coming back into my life. I wanted some reassurance.

The holo played on, and the third experimental result was … evidence of backward time travel! Finally. I wanted to jump, but I restrained myself. My excitement faded away as I remembered that people's memories of these strange experiments had differed before and might differ now, as we viewed this holo. I was suddenly ashamed, for I had put Kitt second. Having seen her crushed twice before, I didn't want her to go through that a third time.

I made myself look at Kitt, to see how she was doing. Her breathing was regular and smooth, her face relaxed. She'd removed her hand from my shoulder and her arms hung loose at her sides.

"What's this all about?" Turen said to me. "You have clear evidence of backward time travel. What is it you intend to do?" He circled about me as if I were his prey. I made no attempt to follow him. "You know I have already published my paper detailing our first experiments and that we never once had a case of backward time travel. What are you trying to do? Are you going to publish this? Show everybody I was wrong?" He wagged a finger in my face and resumed his walk around me. "How did you manage this? We had hundreds of results showing not a single case of backward time travel! You … you come along and get evidence of time travel to the past on your third try?! What are you up to?"

Kitt was shaking her head. She raised her arms and hands at her sides, palms up, and fingers spread apart. "What are you talking about? Are you seeing things? The holo showed quite clearly that no signal arrived, and no backward time travel occurred in this experiment. So why are you saying it did? Are you trying to give Ben a hard time, or — "

"Me? Me give him a hard time? Bahhh!" he cried as he threw his head backward. He pointed his finger at Kitt, and then again at me. "You two are in this together. I just have to figure out … how you did this. Messed with my holo-recorder."

There was nothing further I needed to do, so, as they continued arguing, I just turned away and let them go at it.

All this time, these four days, I had been working very hard to suppress a thought that I no longer needed to bury. In the back of my mind, I had been wondering if I was hallucinating, or something like that. But I had kept it from my conscious thoughts. Occam's razor: the simplest theory is usually the right one. The easiest way to explain all that I had seen, before this bit with Turen showing us the holo, was simply to say that I was imagining things, or the equivalent. I was free from that now. Turen, no matter how much I disliked him, had saved me. He too saw the evidence of backward time travel. I knew then that it wasn't just in my head. With that thought, I was brought back to having to face my childhood monsters, for they were real too.

The very thought of them took hold of me. *They're coming! Anytime now!* My hands started shaking and my legs turned to sponge. My stomach twisted.

Their imminent arrival was another reason I had wanted Turen to see what I had witnessed, to see what had really happened. Now I knew I truly did have some ability, some power, to select what would become real out of all the possibilities. I'd somehow used that skill to erase Kitt's memory of the experiments with backward time travel. If only there were time enough to harness this ability!

Turen had his hand on his hip, was bent forward toward Kitt, his finger shaking in the air. Kitt tapped her lower lip with her hand, and then waved the other side to side as she shook her head. I left Kitt and Turen sparring, and moved to the couch on the other side of the room. I started to feel dizzy. Stress? That's what any medical doctor would say. So much stress in these past four days. And no sleep. The swirling grew. I lost my balance and found my body sinking into the sofa.

Kitt and Turen were too involved to notice me, but

I certainly paid attention to them. They moved as if they were in molasses. Their words were dragged out. No, that couldn't be right. It must have been me, seeing them in slow motion. They continued moving at a reduced pace until they were almost still.

Queasy, I fell off the couch onto my hands and knees. I broke into a cold sweat. I looked up at Kitt and Turen and now they were frozen, neither moving nor speaking. A sharp stab of panic hit me. Then, all around me, things began to fade. A heavy murkiness grew, and it got darker and darker. I could barely see Kitt and Turen. All about hung a dreary gray fog. Gripped by a sudden, deep coldness, I fell into this darkness, and I waited for the inevitable collapse into unconsciousness.

It never came. "Kitt! Turen!" There was only silence. I could make out nothing in this dim fog. I blinked, and blinked again. What was happening to me? I called again, several times. Silence. Darkness.

I lost my sense of up and down. I wobbled on my hands and knees. I turned over on my side, and drifted down to the floor. I got up gradually and noticed that there was indeed gravity, however weak. It was like being in water, but without any feeling of equilibrium. I managed to get to my hands and knees again, and then tried to stand up. I had to move carefully. Now standing, I spread my arms about me, so as not to fall. I blinked, screwed my knuckles over closed eyes, looked and blinked again. Still, I saw just the gloomy darkness of the gray fog. The air was thin and I gasped, taking deep breaths to get enough oxygen.

A dim light grew around me.

Two thin, tall shapes began to emerge from the black ocean. I shuddered at these horribly familiar forms. I could now make out their thin, long limbs, and huge heads. The fog was consumed by the brightening light. I noticed it came from beneath me, that I was standing on a surface that was like translucent glass. When I looked up they were much closer and I saw limbs that glistened like slime and bloated heads.

They had come for me again.

"Greetings, Artemit," said the taller one.

I stiffened. They knew me by name? "Who are you? What do you want? Where am I?" My voice cracked and I struggled to control myself. I only now noticed that I'd taken a step away from them.

"I am Belonthar. This is Merthab. We have brought you here so you might help us." It extended its upper limbs — arms, I suppose — in front of it. The other, Merthab, raised its limbs so its elbows were above its shoulders. I had seen this gesture in the lab! They looked at one another and twittered in high-pitched shrills. Merthab lowered its arms.

What were they saying?

"Help you?" I asked. "Help you with what?"

"Artemit," said Belonthar, the taller of the two. "You are *One Who Chooses*. We ask you to choose us."

I knew what it meant by 'One Who Chooses.' I decided to use this opportunity to learn something more about them, so I asked, "What do you mean, that I am 'The One Who Chooses?' What do I choose?"

Belonthar, arms still open, moved them gently up

and down and said, "You are *One Who Selects* what will become of what might be. We are *Ones Who Might Be*."

The other, Merthab, raised its elbows again and moved close to Belonthar. They turned and twittered again. Then they looked at me and Belonthar said, "We believe that you know of your powers, that you know that you can choose. Is this so, Artemit?"

Out of all the possible outcomes, I was able to select a single one, and that became my reality. If I wanted, I could make it become another person's reality. These were the powers they knew I had and they wanted me to choose for them. "It is so," I admitted, closing and opening my eyes. "I can choose. Somewhat." A thought occurred to me and I asked, "What is it about me that makes me 'The One Who Chooses?'"

More chirping and movements of their limbs, followed by some gasps that meant ... something.

"Artemit," said Belonthar, as it held its mouth in a manner that made me think it was smiling, "do you think you are the only one with this power?"

Blood flushed my cheeks. These beings were not calling me 'The One Who Chooses.' They were calling me 'one of those who can choose.' Of all people, I should have known I was not unique. In the infinite number of multiple universes, there would be an infinite number of people, or beings, who would have the ability to choose. I was not special. I just happened to be one of an infinite number (but a small fraction) who had this power. I almost laughed. "Why me? Why not one of the infinite others who could choose

for you whatever you want? What is it that you want?"
Another thought came to me and I scratched my head.
I hoped to learn more. I asked, "Why is it that one of
your own kind cannot choose?"

They spoke in their language. Merthab took a step
toward me.

"We cannot do this ourselves, but you, Artemit, can
do this for us. We found that you could do this when
you were younger, but we lost our link with you."

A string of expletives burst out of me. I gesticulated
wildly. "Do you have any idea what my life has been
like because of you? The fear I faced as a child? You
came for me every night! You ... monsters!" I flung
more colorful language their way, until I was exhausted and out of breath.

Belonthar was sliding the long fingers of its right
hand over one another. Its eye-slits were closed.
Merthab put its upper limbs on its head. "Your fear,"
Merthab said, "was miniscule compared to the need of
all of our kind. We did not intend to frighten you. Your
powers are strong. That is why you saw us. Take note
of this, Artemit: you saw us. Many others did not. That
is why we selected you."

Belonthar opened its eye-slits and took two steps
toward me. "You are the only one who can do this for
us, Artemit."

Their answers didn't convince me. I was uneasy
about this issue of choosing. There is no logical explanation for what I thought then, but I knew that I would
not, must not, help them.

Images of Kitt flashed through my mind. I needed

to get back to my world. I had to learn more. "Who are you and what is it you want me to choose for you? Tell me why I should do anything for you."

"We are *Ones Who Might Be*," said Belonthar.

"You said that already." I pressed my lips tightly together and swept my arm through the air. "What do you mean?" I folded my arms across my chest.

"You should know. You exist in one of the infinity of multiple universes. You came to be because choices were made that brought you from having a possible existence, to an actual existence." It hesitated, and then whispered, "Do you not recall?"

I rubbed my hands over my head, scratching roughly. I shook my head rapidly from side to side. "Why all the riddles?" I asked. "What am I supposed to remember?"

Belonthar's eye-slits expanded. It spoke louder than it had before. "It doesn't matter, Artemit." Then it moved both of its upper limbs quickly up and down several times. "Make us real."

None of Belonthar's statements made sense to me. They are aliens, I reminded myself.

"Do you truly believe that you, here in this place, do not actually exist?" I asked Belonthar. "That you merely have a possibility of existing?"

Its eye-slits relaxed. It whispered, "It is so."

"No. That makes no sense. If you only have the possibility of existing, how can you even talk to me, if I actually exist and you do not?"

Merthab ran swiftly toward me. It raised its elbow high above its head, and it thrust the rest of its limb toward my face. I flinched. Then Merthab dropped its limb, brought its face close to mine, opened its eye-slits, and looked deep into my eyes. A terrible grin grew on its face, and the slits in its eyes opened even wider. The stink of its breath almost made me gag. It said: "Just as you, *One Who Chooses*, can act upon those of us that might come to exist, Artemit, so too can we act upon you. Indeed, how could it be otherwise? You can make us be. We can affect you. Proof of that is that you are here, in a place of what might become."

My eyes watered from the foul stench. It backed off a bit and the grin faded.

"All you have to do is bring us into being," said Merthab. It moved farther away from me.

I looked at Belonthar. "Surely you exist in one of the multiple universes, Belonthar. Even more, you exist in an infinite number of the multiple universes. So why do you need to be brought into being? *You already exist.* Think about it. We know backward time travel exists. We know that the infinity of multiple universes exists. Time travel experiments have proven it. Therefore, anything that can exist, no matter how unlikely, as long as it is possible, does exist. That means that you already exist. So this is not a place of 'potentially existing,' or whatever you call it."

Something I'd said had just made a huge impact. They chirped in a frantic manner that they hadn't before, and their limbs jerked severely.

Merthab spread its arms and stepped up to me.

"We do *not* exist. We *do* want to exist! You can give this to us!" It yelled.

I took a step back. "What," I paused, and turned to look Belonthar directly in its eyes, "will happen as a consequence if I bring you into existence?"

"Nothing!" Belonthar said, in an uncharacteristically loud voice. "We will simply move into our own world, a real world. That is all. Nothing more!"

Had it been Merthab who had spoken, I might not have taken this shouting as seriously. I thought momentarily that perhaps they were stupid creatures. I again reminded myself that they were not human beings, so I couldn't expect them to act as human beings. Maybe I shouldn't trust my reading of them. But, no, I did trust my instincts. I knew they were lying about something.

I sensed that there would be a terrible disaster if I made them real. I wouldn't do it; I would not help them. This decision was my turning point.

Still, I needed to know more. "What is your potentially real world?"

Belonthar replied. "We are, like you, beings of Earth, another Earth. We are what one type of dinosaur would have evolved into, had they not become extinct, had the asteroid not struck that world."

All along these monsters had looked familiar. They were not just my childhood monsters. I had seen them somewhere else before. I had seen beings like these in an anthology of speculations by scientists, speculations based on known facts, but without the rigor required for discourse. There was a Canadian scientist who had suggested what this line of dinosaurs might have evolved into if they hadn't been wiped out 65 million years ago. I later found that this type of dinosaur was called *Stenonychosaurus*. It had the beginnings of an opposable appendage (a thumb, so to speak), binocular vision, a relatively upright posture, and a relatively large brain. I remembered an illustration that looked quite a bit like these beings, but with a chilling difference. Belonthar and Merthab were much like the evolved *Stenonychosaurus* but, taken to an extreme, they were repulsive.

If that asteroid hadn't struck the Earth, humans wouldn't exist. Belonthar and Merthab were trying to hide something from me. Perhaps they believed that if I chose for them to exist, this universe we lived in would branch over to one where dinosaurs had never become extinct, and where humans had never come to be. Such an extreme change made no sense to me. It seemed like some sort of echo going back 65 million years and coming forward to the present. I don't believe the past can be changed like that but I couldn't convince myself, not completely. I thought that it might be possible that if I brought them from being 'Ones Who Might Be' into existence, they might replace humans. We might cease to exist.

This odd idea went against all that I knew about backward time travel, the infinity of multiple universes, and the idea that you cannot change the past. Yet I could not shrug it off. I knew I must not make these creatures real.

I looked up at them again. Despite all I had been through as a child, I felt sorry for them now. They were intelligent beings that had evolved from dinosaurs, or, at least, that could have.

"Artemit. What is your decision?" Belonthar asked.

I had no choice now but to tell them.

"Find yourselves another 'One Who Chooses.' I won't do it."

Stunned, they neither twittered nor moved.

"Are you certain?" Belonthar asked me.

I told it I was.

The muscles on Merthab's face twitched. It said, "Enough!" It looked at Belonthar, and said in a low voice, "I told you this would not work."

Belonthar stepped toward Merthab, shook its shoulder, and said something in their language.

Merthab shrugged off Belonthar's grip. It looked at me and said, "Watch what will happen now to your arms, Artemit."

My arms were bare; I was wearing a short-sleeved shirt. I extended them in front of me. Everything seemed fine. A strange tingling enveloped my skin. It grew warm. The hairs on my arms and hands started to smoke, and continued to do so until all the hair was gone. The heat intensified. My skin was practically on fire. I screamed. "Stop this!"

Belonthar shrieked something to Merthab, its limbs flying through the air. It continued its extreme gestures and spoke frenetically, but was ignored by Merthab.

The pain was becoming unbearable. "Stop! Stop." My fingers started to spasm. My skin had turned a deep red. I waved my arms frantically.

"Make us real Artemit," said Merthab. "Then the pain will go away."

My skin bubbled. Tears filled my eyes. I gritted my teeth, knowing what was coming, helpless to prevent it.

Why not just do as they asked? I still had reservations, but ... the pain, and the thought of how far Merthab might go...

I want to tell you that I resisted. But I cannot. I broke. I tried to speak, but could not! My skin boiled away. My arms were a mess of red and sticky tissue.

Suddenly the torture ceased.

There was no damage. My skin, hairs and all, was back. I felt no pain.

Belonthar said something to Merthab, who then jerked one of its arms up and down. Belonthar's head dropped and its eye-slits closed.

"Artemit," said Belonthar, almost lethargically, "I must ask you one last time. Will you make us real?"

I attempted to speak, but again was immobile.

Belonthar looked at Merthab. Merthab nodded its head sharply. Belonthar then turned toward me, tilted its head down a bit, and spoke quietly.

"I regret what we must now do, Artemit. We must try another way."

Merthab glanced at Belonthar, then faced me and said, "There is only one other way." Stepping toward me, Merthab added, "You should have cooperated. Now we have to do this."

I wanted to say that I would cooperate, but I was still frozen.

"We will remove your brain. We will use it to generate thoughts that will be close to those you would have thought voluntarily. In this manner, we might still come to be."

I couldn't believe what I had just heard.

Abruptly, they turned, and started walking away.

Though my hands were shaking, I could not help but ask myself: *Why are they leaving?* With that thought, my immobility vanished. Ideas came to me quickly, and with precision. Understanding flooded through me, so satisfying that what I would say and do next would be effortless.

"Merthab. Belonthar. Stop," I said. They stopped.

"Turn around and come back." They did.

I walked toward Merthab. My face in front of its, I whispered, "You blundered." Still focused on Merthab, I said, "So did you, Belonthar. Not as badly, but enough.

"You said I didn't remember, Belonthar. You burned my arms, Merthab." I held them up. "They seem just fine now."

Merthab started to speak. I passed my hand smoothly across its face. "You are an embarrassment to your kind," I said.

I swept my arms around me, my head turning from left to right. "All of this. This place of fog. Your would-be world. It's a lie."

"No, Artemit," said Belonthar.

"Oh, your world exists. You are in it, but I'm not. I'm still on the floor, beside my couch. Kitt and Turen are with me, probably trying to help me. They didn't slow down. You simply drew my mind away from them.

"Did you think," I swung my gaze to Merthab, "that you could actually make me think my arms were burning without giving yourselves away?" I touched my finger to my temple. "This is the only place where you are, in any sense, real. You can affect me, *but only because I believe in you.* Just as I did as a child."

Merthab attempted to approach me. Without thinking, I held up a hand. It halted, swayed, and dropped to its knees.

"You do live in a would-be world. You connected with me when I was a boy, and you lost me when I was convinced you were just in my head. You got me back when we did the quantum experiments. My mind opened to you again.

"You tried for me in the lab, but Kitt was there and I wouldn't let you in. I'm not sure how I kept you away. Not quite. Then you took me when Kitt was safe and I had only myself to think of."

I looked at Belonthar. "You can't take my brain. All you can do is affect my thoughts." I looked at Merthab, still on its knees. "You made my arms burn. But only in my mind. You took the risk that I would break. When I did not, you gave up your secrets. Belonthar tried to stop you, but you went too far."

Belonthar clasped its hands under its chin. "Artemit," it pleaded, "we ask only that you make us real."

"You do ask. Yes. I am *the only one* you can ask. I am

93

the only *real* mind that you can connect with." I leaned toward Belonthar. "Isn't that right?" I whispered.

Belonthar tilted its head down and spread its arms at its sides. "Since you know all this, why not now grant us what we ask for?"

"Because you blundered."

Its eyes met mine.

"What is it I don't remember?"

Belonthar's mouth opened and closed. Twice.

"You won't tell me, will you?"

Belonthar's eye-slits relaxed.

"I can choose you to be real, but I can't choose you to be any *less* real than you are now. You *do* live in a quantum world, where nothing is ever real, and only possibilities exist."

Later, I couldn't help but wonder what that would be like. What would our whole encounter be like for them? Had they experienced every possible way this discussion could unfold, yet none was real?

"If I had the ability to reduce your state of existence, to make it impossible for you to become real, I would use that skill and eliminate you completely."

Merthab stood. "But you don't, Artemit. We will not give up. You will still believe in us. You cannot change that. We'll come for you again. As many times as it takes."

"Yes. I do believe in you again. I wish I didn't. I *will* find a way to stop believing in you."

Belonthar stepped forward. "It is too late, Artemit. We can now arrange for others to make us real." It moved its mouth in the manner it had before, when I'd thought it had smiled.

I turned and walked away. The fog came up, but this time it was I who made it appear.

I lay down and closed my eyes. My sense of weight gradually returned. The air was thicker and I breathed normally.

I heard a distant cry. It became louder. It was Kitt's voice calling my name. I opened my eyes, my hands reaching for her face.

She pulled me toward her in a warm embrace. She hugged me tighter and all my muscles relaxed. "Al and I were arguing," Kitt said, "and I didn't notice what was happening to you, until … it was too late and I … we couldn't do anything!"

"What happened to me? What did you see, Kitt?"

"You were still here, but," she moved her finger in a circle, "not really here. You seemed dazed, and, oh, this is going to sound incredible…" She rapidly tapped her chin with one finger. "I could touch you, and feel you, just like now, but, you were … soft, somehow, not solid like you are now. You were mumbling and rolling, and getting up on your hands and knees and then standing and swaying, turning and muttering. You put your arms out and started to cry and scream. We tried to calm you down. Tried to talk to you. But you wouldn't answer us. We called to you and shook you. You went on and on … until you just curled up. We had to check your pulse, you were so still, and then … you weren't soft anymore, you'd become solid again. Ben, please tell me what happened."

Kitt had said "we" and only then did I remember Turen. I looked at him. He was flopped out on the other sofa. He was pale, and there was absolutely no expression on his face. He stared into some empty pit, oblivious to Kitt and me.

"What's happened to him?" I asked Kitt.

Kitt pressed her hand on my chest and said, "Ben, tell me what happened to you." She took my face in her hands and pulled me close to her. "Please!"

I sat up, put my hands on my head, and closed my eyes. I said, "Kitt ... it's so strange..." I told her what I had experienced.

She sat very still, and finally said, "How will we stop them?"

"I will not allow them to use me. Even when I tried to give them what they wanted, I could not. We need to find out: who are the others that they now can use to make them real?"

"How can we do that?"

"I don't know." Then I remembered. I pointed at Turen. "What happened to him?"

Before Kitt could reply, Turen broke out of his trance and looked at me. There was something in his eyes; he had seen ... something. His face was almost gray and was covered with sweat. He breathed shallowly, and spoke so quietly that I could only just hear him and I strained to capture every word.

"I ... I saw them." Turen swallowed. "Kitt saw you, but I saw you and the two of them." He paused, his eyes unfocused. "I saw the ... I saw the time travel experiments. I mean, I didn't see them on the holo, not at first. Kitt kept asking me what was the matter with me. Why I didn't see what she saw. And then ... then..." Blood drained from his face. "And then I saw what Kitt saw! But I still remember what I saw before, I mean, when I first looked at the holo..." He looked at us, alternating between us, as if trying to figure out which of us could explain to him what had happened. "But now," he continued, "when I look at the holo I just see what Kitt saw all along."

It was as I had feared.

Abruptly, Turen stood, whirled, and yelled, "What's happening? What is going on? None of this makes any sense! I see two different things in the holo and Kitt sees the same thing all the time. And you, standing and speaking while ... while they moved around you ... until they faded away and you ... came back. What is ... How can I make any sense of this?" He sat down.

"Maybe I can. First, though, tell me, in detail, what they looked like."

After he had described them, I knew he had indeed seen Belonthar and Merthab. They were no longer confined within my mind!

Al Turen had seen not only the proof that backward time travel did occur, but also the monsters. I had to decide. I could either have both, or neither.

I knelt in front of Kitt and took her face in my hands. Her blue eyes asked me questions. I kissed her, a gentle kiss.

I focused on Turen and made my choice.

He rolled off the couch, and looked around the room. He rubbed his fingers over his eyes, and glanced around again. "What am I doing here? What's going on?"

"You came here to show us the holo," said Kitt.

He frowned and said, "Oh, yeah, the experiments you did. Confirming what we already knew."

Kitt's brow furrowed and she searched my eyes. I touched my lips with my finger. Her frown died.

I motioned toward the door. "It's late, Al. Go home. Celebrate some more."

Kitt and I considered our options, desperately seeking solutions. We had a lot of thinking to do, but right now had nothing more to say. We moved closer and held one another.

THE BIRD

\\\\\\\\\\\\\\\\\\\\\\\\\\\\

It was a mild spring morning, with a clear sky and a gentle breeze. The chirping of birds filled the air. Jill Turner saw and heard none of it. She walked at a steady pace, gazing at the path in front of her. Lost in thought, she trudged along. She was thinking about the topic of her essay, and she thought about the title for the hundredth time. *What is the Meaning of Being*? Indeed, she wondered, what is the point of it all? Why should I bother to finish this essay, or to finish this Master's degree, or to do anything at all? Why should I be doing this essay, of all days, on a Sunday?

The doubt had come upon her suddenly and inexplicably. Once it had taken hold of her, it wouldn't let go. Her friends and some of the more perceptive of her instructors were worried. None of them knew what was bothering her, but they all knew that it was something serious.

Jill's long brown hair bounced gracefully as she walked. A touch of makeup brought out the gold flecks in her green eyes. She wore a soft pink sweater, black slacks, and a snug beige jacket. Her thoughts were in quite another state.

Jill made her way down the path to the side door of the philosophy building, took out her key, and let herself in. The building had that dead feeling that she dreaded so much. The door swung shut behind her, and she stopped. What is the meaning of being? She raised her right hand, pressed her fingers on her temple, and looked down the hallway, focusing on the door to the department library. Why bother to go there, to read the books and the passages, to write this essay? Motionless, she stood there for some time. She turned back to the door, reaching out for the knob. She could leave the building and forget all this nonsense.

Her hand dropped to her side. She moved toward the library, put her key into the keyhole, hesitated, and then turned the handle and went inside.

Mechanically, she took from the shelves the books and journals she needed. She placed them on the table in front of her, took out her pen and writing pad. Leaning back in the chair, she folded her arms. She stared at nothing and time drifted by.

The sound of fluttering broke her from her reverie. She turned around to face the stacks. Jill strained her ears. She heard outdoor sounds through an open window: people talking and laughing, cars driving, birds singing. But the library was silent. Then she heard the flapping sound again. Curious, she stepped up from the chair and listened hard. Again, fluttering, coming from the back of the room. Noiselessly, she tiptoed down an aisle between the stacks of books. This time she both saw and heard.

It was a tiny bird, perched on an empty place between books on one of the shelves, trapped in this room. For a while she simply stood and watched the bird. Suddenly, it lifted off and disappeared.

Jill's stomach quivered. She stroked both sides of her forehead with her fingertips. "Please," she whispered, "please let me help this bird." She walked quietly down to the end of the aisle, searching for the bird. She heard it again and knew she was close. Looking down the next aisle she spotted the poor creature, which had alighted on another empty spot on one of the shelves. Its wings beat frantically.

She approached the bird hesitantly, but it took flight and disappeared over the stack, near the wall with the open window. Jill followed. "Hello," she cooed. "Please let me help you. I won't hurt you."

The bird tilted its head as she approached. Jill put her hands together, palms up, and spoke again. "Here. Come here. I'll let you out. You can trust me."

She inched her way, held her breath, and placed her hands just below the bird. "Here. Come here." Jill felt tiny beads of perspiration on her forehead.

The bird stepped into Jill's open palms.

She walked slowly toward the window. It was tilted with the top inward, and she moved her hands, the bird safely nestled in her palms, toward the gap.

"There!" she whispered. "Now you can go."

The bird looked up at her, then toward the outside air, then back to Jill. It flew out the window.

The corners of her mouth turned up ever so slightly as she picked up her pen and started to write.

THE TORTURE

\\\\\\\\\\\\\\\\\\\\\\\\\\\\\\\\\\\\\\

Going to the convenience store at 3:00 a.m. was a stupid thing to do. I knew it and went anyway. I would never have allowed my children to do this, but I'd be all right, I told myself. In and out and back home to finish the movie.

After selecting my snacks, I waited at the till. The owner was rearranging canned goods on one of the shelves, taking too long. The fingers of my right hand pressed into my palm and I rubbed my thumb over my forefinger. I cleared my throat. The man came. I paid him and scurried out of the building. Only heartbeats later, I heard footfalls behind me, and glanced over my shoulder to see someone gaining on me, a big man who could overpower me easily.

He started to trot.

I ran as fast as I could down the sidewalk, but the smacking of his boots grew louder. I sensed that he was right behind me, cut left onto the street, and came to a quick stop. He skidded past me, reversed, and charged toward me. Now I had to run the other way, away from home. I raced down the street. Again he caught up to me. I halted abruptly and broke to my right. He slid by.

This would be my last chance. Adrenaline rushed

through me and I ran harder than I would have thought possible. I heard the pounding of his feet fade away, and thought I was free.

I had to know where he was. Continuing toward sanctuary, now scurrying backwards, I observed that he was nowhere near. I would never repeat this mistake, I told myself.

Thick arms wrapped around me as I bounced off his hard chest. It shouldn't have been possible. I'd lost him!

"I've got you now, little boy," he whispered, his breath hot in my ear. "Wait till you find out what I'm gonna do to you."

I struggled, twisting, turning, writhing, using strength I'd never had before, but it was futile.

Suddenly, his left hand moved up and I found myself breathing through a moist rag, drawing in a medicinal smell that sent me into a world of black. My last thoughts were of my wife, son, and daughter, safe and sound asleep at home.

When I woke, I was in a chair. My wrists and ankles were attached to the arms and legs of the chair with several loops of duct tape. I could not move. My vision cleared. On a shiny metal tray almost touching my chest, I saw tools and instruments. My heart thumped as I took in the pliers and short pieces of thick wire that had been sharpened to points. In front of me were scissors, hammers, knives, and metal devices with designs I would never have conceived. Cold sweat dripped from my chin.

I heard a buzzing sound. The guy held an electric knife.

"Hello, little boy. Time to play."

The knife came closer to me. I pressed myself into the chair, wishing I could pass through it and out the other side. The noise of the motor died down, replaced by a hideous chuckling. I turned my face to find three people sitting in chairs, off to my side, watching, laughing.

"Help me!" I gasped, but they simply exchanged glances.

The whining abruptly became much louder.

It moved toward me.

I shouted, cried, wept, and begged. The laughter of these three psychos reverberated in my ears.

I closed my eyes and screamed.

The buzzing grew louder, then just stopped.

My eyes opened and I saw myself sitting in the chair. But from *outside*. The spectators were still staring. The torturer was working. Cries of anguish continued. Maniacal laughter.

What was going on? Was I hallucinating?

It was almost unbearable to witness this senseless infliction of pain, yet I could not do otherwise. The members of the audience—sick people, monsters themselves—were enjoying the show. The madman went about his business as if it were an art. I writhed and howled. Yet I felt nothing.

"You're not there anymore."

Now a voice was added to my illusory world. It

had spoken only once. But that had made me peer toward it, to find out to whom the voice belonged.

I then became aware that I was in another body. I could see, and was able to move my head. I raised my arms, examined the palms of my hands, and flexed my fingers.

"You're safe now," the man beside me said.

"I know you're not real," I insisted. "I'm dreaming."

"That's not so. You know it. You are thinking the way you did —" he tilted his head toward the torture chamber, "—before."

"I'm still back there."

He folded his arms across his chest. "You doubt what you have just said."

That was true. I *wasn't* sure. Who was this man?

"I am part of what you call 'God.' "

"You're God?"

He lifted a finger. "Part of."

"People stopped believing in God a long time ago. Less than one percent still believe. It's been that way since the 2050s."

He pointed at me. "That doesn't mean God doesn't exist." With the slightest trace of a smile, but a sadness evident in his glistening eyes, he added, "None of your religions were right about God."

"Then what is God?"

"You might find out."

I wanted to hear more, but would not ask.

"If there is a God, tell me why God would —" I

stopped, realizing that I was talking to a person in a dream.

I looked around me for the first time. I could see the torture chamber and what was happening there, but from the outside, as if one wall was missing. Nothing but darkness surrounded that room. I could see the arms and legs of my new body, and the man whom I was imagining as well. I was not surprised when I noticed that he was dressed in a white shirt and wore white pants. His hair was light blond and short. There was nothing in his appearance that stood out. Except for the room and the two of us, there was only blackness.

"Why God would...?"

All right; why not? I decided to go along with it. I closed my right hand, ran my thumb up and down my finger, and continued, "Would permit this torment to go on?"

He shook his head.

"Would allow serial killers," I continued. "Murder, rape, all the evils in the world? Why let all of this happen?"

"God does not allow these things."

"It's going on right now! It's been going on for thousands of years!"

"True."

"Well then, why doesn't God step in and put an end to these evils?"

"God does so when possible. Do you think God would do nothing to prevent such atrocities if it were possible to prevent them?"

106

I considered his question.

"What do you suppose has happened to you?" he asked.

"Me? What do you call that?" I pointed. He kept his gaze on me. "That man is tormenting me. Hear the screams? See the blood? And, what about the sickos watching, and liking what they see? Tell me: why allow that to go on?"

"I've told you: it isn't 'allowed.' You've been taken away from that horror."

As if it had been planned, my voice—or the voice of the body tied to the chair—cried out, "It's not him in here! It's me! Stop him!"

The spectators simply grinned.

I was puzzled. How could I be *in* my body, experience no pain, say what I just had, hear it from the *outside*, and still be in my imaginary world?

"How can you explain the words we are hearing?" he asked.

"It's all in my head. I'm not out here. I'm in that chair, in agony—"

"You are here now. You do not suffer. You have been spared that nightmare."

I thought about that, and then spoke. "Suppose I have. What about my wife? How's she going to feel when they find my dead body? What about my children? What's God going to do to help them? My parents, my brothers and sisters, my friends. How does sparing me this pain and torment help them?"

He looked down. "God does what can be done but

cannot do everything. It is possible to save you, but no more than that. You are not suffering right now."

"Oh? Then who is?"

For the second time, we heard my voice shout. "Get me out of here! We've been switched!"

"I think you know who," he said.

I took my time before replying. "If the torturer is in my body, who's in his?"

"He is."

I almost laughed. "*He* is? So he's in *both*?"

"Yes."

"Both," I said. "So he's enjoying hacking himself up, but he's not too keen about being tortured. If what you said were true, he'd simply quit."

"You're still thinking like you used to."

"All right, then. Tell me why he keeps mutilating himself."

"Can't you figure it out?"

My imagination was hard at work. I decided to keep playing the game. "He can't control his hands. He's not aware of inflicting the pain that he is, but he's *feeling* all the pain."

He nodded.

"I don't believe it."

"Why not? Suppose it is as I've said. What are things like for him?"

"He's experiencing what he has done to me, what he's probably done many times before."

"What is his situation now? What is happening to him because of his evil nature?"

After thinking for a while, I finally absorbed his point.

"Yes, he is experiencing the beginning of something that is like what you call 'Hell.'"

If it were so, what a fitting Hell that would be. I suddenly wondered why God, or a part of God, would be having a discussion with me, and I asked, "Why is it so important to you that I believe?"

His eyes fixed on me and did not waver.

I could not hold his gaze.

"You already know the answer to that question."

I took some time before responding. My eyes swung between the room my physical body was in, and the man — the 'Part of God' — at my side. I said, "Convince me. Show me why I should believe."

He folded his arms across his chest and moved toward me until we were almost touching. Again, I couldn't look him in the eye. He spoke very quietly. "You know that nothing can convince you. No matter what I do, or tell you, you can always say that it is in your mind." He didn't even blink. "Let me ask you this.

"Do you *really believe*," he raised a finger, "that you are in your own body," he raised a second finger, "you are talking as if your torturer is in your body," and a third, "that all of this with me is in your mind," a fourth, "and you feel no pain. Do you really believe that this is what is *actually happening* right now?"

I refused to reply.

"You already have everything you need to decide, and it is for you to decide, not for me to convince you."

I couldn't believe it, started to say so, and—

—I returned to the chair.

In a split second, I had gone from a painless world to a torment that words cannot convey.

The monster in front of me put down his instrument, patted his thighs and chest, glanced at the others, and said, "I'm … here…" He brought his hands to his face, ran his palms over his cheeks. "I'm OK now."

He reached for the tool he'd been using, hesitated, then dropped his arms to his sides.

Pulsations of pain. Blood. My chin fell to my chest. My eyes closed. I took one last breath.

Time crawled, the last second of my life stretching on as if it was longer than my entire life. Like water bursting from a shattered dam, my thoughts surged furiously in this final shred of time, infinitely faster than ever before in my life. I thought every single thought that I was capable of thinking.

I was out again.

"We almost lost you."

"What comes next?" I asked.

"Follow me," was the reply.

And I did.

THE HOLE

\\\\\\\\\\\\\\\\\\\\\\\\\\\\

I'd thought I was ready. But now, as I hung above the hole, about to drop into it, to leave and possibly never come back, I was sweating and I couldn't breathe.

Behind me were the space vessel *Sol-III* and the far side of the moon. The hole orbited the Earth at the same rate as the moon, always directly above the lunar surface, and never visible from Earth.

What beings had made this enigma? Why had it been placed here, hidden from us, waiting to be discovered?

The captain of the *Sol-III* asked me for the third time if I was ready to go, and I shivered as I broke out of my reverie.

"Yes, yes, I'm fine," I replied. "I just need a minute here."

"Roger that. Standing by."

The mouth of the hole was wide open, ready to take me in. *Get a grip*, I told myself.

We had made every attempt to learn about this hole, studied it from all sides, and with every method we knew. It had an opening on the side facing the moon, but it could not even be seen from the other side. It was so small that the ellipsoidal cage we had built around it was merely the size of a large boulder.

No wonder it had taken us so long to find it, and accidentally at that.

We had plenty of theories, but not many hard facts. Our probing into the hole had been limited to only about fifty meters inside of it. We had no idea what lay beyond that distance. Nothing that we'd sent into the hole had ever come back, including the robo-probes and the pods carrying the trained monkeys. My going in was our last, desperate attempt to find out what this anomaly was and why it had been put here.

I was both brave and foolish enough to agree to this journey. I had my own special reason for wanting to go. I also knew that what I would find, if I returned, would matter to Kitt. I thought of her now, her long red hair, deep green eyes, and slim figure. I pictured her rolling her eyes when colleagues would make a remark she disagreed with, shaking a fist slightly but unmistakably.

Thinking about Kitt reminded me of my encounter with Raphael Turen the night before. I'd gone to the cafeteria late, finding it empty, as I'd hoped. I'd wanted a relaxing cup of herbal tea and to check my calculations one more time. Lost in thought, I'd barely heard him come in after me.

"If it isn't the great Jared Artemit. What are you doing here?" he asked, as he sat down on the other side of my table.

"Me? I've got a job to do tomorrow," I said, as I pulled my computer toward me. "What are *you* doing here, *Turen*?"

He put his right hand on the side of his neck, tilted

his head back, and looked down his nose at me. "Just come to remind you one more time that it's not going to work." He puffed out a blast of air through his nose. "You're not going to come back, you know. Your theory is wrong. Kitt's got it right." He put his elbows on the table and moved his face close to mine. He was a good foot taller than I. He glared down at me and said, "When you go down that hole, you're gone for good. Why can't you see that?"

I placed my fingertips on the table and elevated myself off my chair. Our eyes level, I said, "You're an *experimentalist*, Turen. You don't understand Kitt's theory or mine, or why they agree on some things and not on others. You—"

"Shut up, Artemit." He leaned back in his chair and began inspecting his fingernails. "I know enough. Maybe I can't add up all your Feynman-Einstein diagrams. So what?" He started to nibble on his thumb. "Kitt says there's no space-time loop that'll bring you back. If there was, you could travel to the past." He looked up at me and flipped his hand toward me. "And that's just stupidity."

I lowered myself back onto my chair, placed my hands flat on the table, and curled my fingers into my palms. I struck the table with the knuckles of my right hand. "I'll be generous and give you an F for thinking like that, Turen. You can't travel to *your own* past. Unless, of course, you already have." He frowned and I wanted to smile. "Kitt's theory doesn't say that I can't return. It just says that if I do, time travel to the past can occur within a single universe. My calculations show that you can also go to the past in another universe. If — no, *when* — I return, that will mean my work can't be ignored anymore." I interwove my fingers and rested my hands on the table.

"You're an idiot, Artemit," he whispered, almost too low to be heard. "Only you and the fools following you believe in these many universes."

"Oh? Then why did the committee decide that I would go? What's bugging *you* is that they didn't allow you to do your experiment." He stiffened and I pressed on. "Your proposal was just a waste of time." I did a mock study of my own fingernails, exaggerating the turning of my hand. "You would have just ruptured the entire set of connected holes. *All* of the theories and *all* of the theorists agree on that. That's what *everyone* thinks of your work. The only reason you've been selected to review my journey is because your father has—"

Turen stood so abruptly that his chair fell backwards with a crash. I could see a vein pulsing at his temple.

I forced myself not to smile.

"Go on your stupid mission, Artemit," he said, as he leaned over me. "And don't come back!"

The captain's hail returned me to the here and now. I realized that if I waited any longer I might change my mind, and I could not do that. What I wanted was in that hole under me, and, suddenly, I *had* to go in.

"I'm on my way," I said, and pushed the bright red lever that sent me down toward the mouth of the hole.

The entry was smooth, the pod shaking ever so slightly. I sent back signals, knowing that after I was a few meters in, nothing would make it back to the *Sol-III*. The lights on the pod lit the inside of the mouth. It was a yellowish brown, and it glistened like slime. The reflected light faded. I moved along and I saw nothing but the inside of the pod.

Gradually, the pod sped up, pressing me back into the seat. The pressure increased as the pod moved faster and faster down the throat of the hole. A slick tingling ran over my entire body. The walls of the tube pressed on the pod, squeezing it inward. The instrument panel flashed rapidly on and off.

Then the pod's lights died. Reaching forward, I groped for the panel, the tips of my fingers finding it. I moved my arms down and found the sides of my seat. A rumbling noise startled me, and I realized that I was hearing myself moaning. Tears filled my eyes and rolled down my cheeks. My jaw ached from gritting my teeth.

Suddenly the pod went out of control, rolling and spinning in all directions. It started to shake and rattle. The pod swung me about so violently that I lost consciousness.

I woke to a motionless calm. Had I stopped, or was I moving at a steady speed? There was no way for me to tell.

Slowly, I closed and opened my eyes, strained my ears, but sensed nothing. My lungs filled as I took a deep breath. Time passed and my body started to quiver. My pulse was up and I was breathing too fast. What had happened to me? Where was I? Was this the end of my trip?

Just when I thought I could take no more immobility, the pod started to shake, and I cried out. Leaning from side to side, I willed the pod to move some more. The rattling changed to a slow vibration, and the pod's lights came back on.

Without warning, the pod spilled out into empty space, and moved smoothly away from the mouth. I stopped the pod. There were stars all around me, and directly ahead was the moon, in a crescent phase.

The *Sol-III* was absent.

Magnified images of the various research sites on the moon's surface were displayed on the monitors next to the panel in front of me. I should have been able to see some of the lights at these locations, but the screens were blank. I attempted to communicate but received no response. Increasing the magnification, I searched again.

The lunar surface was dark and empty.

I turned around and looked back at the hole.

I saw the familiar, roughly circular patch of space that was void of stars. The cage was gone.

* * *

A careful study of the moon's far side surface showed only the smallest of differences, so I took my next step. I set the pod to take me out of the cone behind the moon from which Earth could not be seen.

A faint and diffuse glow was peeking past the limb of the moon. It grew as I traveled on, until I saw clouds in the planet's atmosphere. A while later, I could see the sunlit part of Earth, and more clouds over the land and oceans. Suddenly, I realized that I could have ended up anywhere, in any universe, and that the moon and Earth could have been much different than the ones I had left. I was lucky to be in a place that was so similar to my own.

Soon after that, I saw some of the night side of Earth. More and more of it came into view. Then I realized that I should try making contact with Earth, and I quickly radioed a message. Seconds passed. No reply. I tried several more times on different frequencies. Nothing.

The night side of the world was black. My fingers shook and my space suit was cold. I shivered but went on. Eventually, I moved far enough that I could see the whole half of the Earth that was facing me.

Not a single light. Not one beanstalk. No evidence of people.

My pulse quickened at the thought that perhaps I had gone backward in time. I wondered again if I might be in a different universe, or if I was still in my own but so far back in time that humans did not rule the planet, had not yet built the cage.

The answers would come if I simply carried on to Earth.

Through breaks in the clouds, the magnified images of the surface revealed the absence of cities I had known. I searched over other areas but found no artificial constructs to indicate the existence of intelligent life.

If I had not gone to another universe, I was in the

past of my own. Either way, there was nothing else to do but orbit, study the surface, and possibly land somewhere.

After several revolutions, I had found no indication of intelligent life. There might well be people emerging from a stone age, so I decided to check, just to satisfy my curiosity. I did so, only to find that this world had nothing of the sort, at least not in the places I looked. There were no large life-forms, no creatures even remotely resembling humans or dinosaurs.

That left me with only one thing to do. I headed back toward the hole, frowned at the thought that it might not be there, or that I wouldn't be able to find it. It was exactly where I thought it would be.

Again I hovered above the mouth of the hole, or the funnel as I sometimes called it, but I took some time to reflect before doing anything.

This funnel was at the same co-orbital point as the one I'd gone into, and could never be seen from Earth. The perplexing feature of the hole's distance from the moon was that it was in striking disagreement with Newtonian gravity. We'd had co-orbital satellites that maintained their positions above the far side of the moon, but they were where Newton's laws said they should be, at the 'L2 Lagrange point.' The hole was about ten percent farther out. Still, it was inside the cone behind the moon, so it could not be seen from any point on the Earth's surface. How it could be co-orbital at this distance was something no one had been able to explain. That it was also so small made its discovery almost miraculous.

118

While I had been busy adventuring, the computers had calculated the orbit of the moon around the Earth. The numbers were the same as those for my own pair. The implication was that I *was* in another universe and at almost the exact same time as in mine. I knew this because the distance between the Earth and the moon changes with time. Earlier in time the moon was closer to Earth, and later would be farther away.

If I had traveled in time, it was not by much.

I didn't think of it then, but the pod's computers would have additional detailed information in them, including the continental coastlines and the river systems and lakes of the planet.

I moved my space pod down toward the mouth. For the second time, I journeyed through the funnel. The ride was much smoother. Contrary to my expectations, I did not return to my own universe, but instead emerged from the hole only to find another dead moon, and another Earth with no signs of intelligent life.

After repeating this futile endeavor several times, I wondered if I would ever find another Earth with intelligence upon it.

Realizing that the pod still had plenty of fuel remaining, I took some time to examine information about these Earths and moons I'd visited. All of the moons were near perfect replicas of my own, the Earths less so. Their physical features varied, only slightly, but unequivocally. That agreed with my finding other differences on these planets.

The next version of Earth that I encountered was

dominated by frightening insectoids that resembled nothing I'd ever seen or imagined. I had descended into the atmosphere until I was about a hundred meters above the surface, so I could examine them. These creatures ranged in size from tiny, multi-legged bugs smaller than a spec of dirt to behemoths as large as a human being. The bigger ones seemed always to be aware of me, turning themselves on their many legs to follow the pod as I passed over them. They had claws, pinchers, mandibles, and multi-jointed legs. Their torsos were thin but wide, curving down, and shaped like a spoon. Some were mostly purple, others blue, or yellow. Scattered over their bodies were splotches of other colors so spectacular that they reminded me of colorful drawings in comic books. I could not bring myself to study them in detail, even though I should have. Perhaps their awareness of me was what pushed me away.

On the next world, I encountered intelligent life, and brought the pod near the surface. It had never occurred to me that spiders could be intelligent. Yet I saw their buildings and cities, and watched them holding their writing instruments, putting their strange looking symbols onto paper. I was thinking of leaving them a written message, to tell them about the hole in space on the far side of their moon, but I doubted that they could ever translate my language into theirs. Instead, before I went back into orbit, I left them drawings in the hope they might be of some use, and that the spiders might come to understand what the drawings meant.

The spiders were small creatures, about the size of

my fist. Their main body part was a flattened oval, connected to a smaller, almost spherical head. What intrigued me the most were their legs, if I can call them that. They appeared to have no joints, and were more like a tendril that diminished in size from the base of the body down to the ends. In writing, the spiders wrapped one or more tendrils about their 'pens.' I believe that it was with these tentacles that the spiders had manipulated their environment, much as we had with our opposable fingers and thumbs.

I was thirsty and drank some water, but I had no desire for food.

After leaving the spiders my drawings, all I could do was go back into the hole. I repeated this process over and over again. Even though the pod's energy source was nuclear, I feared I might consume all its energy before I'd find another Earth with intelligent life. In any case, I realized that I'd have to live on one of these other versions of Earth. Maybe I'd find sentient beings to talk to, maybe not. I found it hard to keep looking since, by that point, I had pretty much given up any hope of finding a world that would be an appealing place to live out the rest of my life.

Nevertheless, I went into the funnel once again. Like the first time, this journey was a rough ride. The pod accelerated quickly, and closed in upon me. I fought to catch my breath. Electricity jolted my spine and I cried out. The lights in the pod went out, came back, and blinked off and on. Pressure mounted inside my head. A sharp noise pierced my ears. The pod went out of control, rocking and tumbling. I gripped the sides of my seat and closed my eyes. My body shook as the pod twisted through the funnel. I couldn't adjust to the wild spinning. I blacked out.

This time I dreamed. There were humanoid aliens reaching out for me with their thin, long arms. Their blank faces pleaded with me. They were unpleasant in appearance, their arms and legs too long, their heads too large. I turned from them and ran, as fast and as hard as I could. Each time I glanced back, they were closer to me. I just managed to keep ahead of them.

Soon after I regained consciousness, the readings on the monitors revealed that the other end of the hole was moving rapidly toward me.

Emerging from the funnel, tears swelled in my eyes as I gazed upon the *Sol-III*, half a kilometer away. The lights of the research stations on the far side of the moon were clearly displayed on the monitors.

I was home.

The captain contacted me. "How did you get back so fast?" she asked.

"How long was I gone?"

"About ten minutes."

* * *

After docking the pod, I entered the *Sol-III*. All the people who had worked on this project were there. They shook hands with me and clapped me on my back.

Aware of my sweat-drenched clothing, my scraggy hair, and the stubble on my chin, I went off to shower, shave, and put on fresh clothes. I joined my colleagues for an evening meal. They asked me questions and I answered as many as I could. There was something unsettling about that evening, but I wasn't quite sure what. I would find out all too soon. Excusing myself early, I went off to my quarters, slumped on my bed, and —

— I was back in the funnel, with the spiders and insectoids crammed with me inside the pod. The two species were intertwined. The spiders were half as big as I was, and had jagged mouths and claws, which they used to hold spears. They jabbed at me and pierced my body, blood soaking my clothes. Dozens of rat-sized insectoids crawled over my neck and shoulders. Their tendrils wrapped around my neck and squeezed so tightly that I couldn't breathe. Other tentacles circled my head and drew my face toward their ugly, foul mouths. Restrained, I squirmed and thrashed as they prepared to bite chunks of flesh from my face. I squeezed my eyes shut and felt slithering tentacles on my eyelids. Something was prying into my nose. I blew out forcefully.

I was relieved to wake at that point. Later, I fell back into a shallow sleep, haunted by more dreams that took me into and out of the hole.

* * *

The next day, I sat at the table in the meeting room in Raphael Turen's office, waiting for him. His job was to review my trip. This was his big moment, and he would try to milk it. I had other plans. He finally arrived, fifteen minutes late. When he did show up, he took a seat without acknowledging my presence. His attention was on his hand as he stroked his thumb over his forefinger briefly. His thumb rolled over his next finger, then the ring finger, and finally the pinky received attention. Still not looking at me, he lilted, "How was your trip?" and returned to his examination of his fingers and thumb.

I put my palms on the table and my fingers curled up. "It's all in the pod's computers. You should know all about it."

He wore a smug smile on his face. "That's been done."

I tilted my head to the side and pointed a finger at him. "How much have you yourself looked at? It's over twenty hours long. What parts have you reviewed?"

He put his hand on the table and met my eyes for the first time. "All of it," he said.

"How could you have?" I asked. "Do you mean that you had various people look at different parts, so that you could cover everything?"

Turen took his time before replying.

"All that is recorded is the fifty meters you went into the hole, and the same fifty meters of you coming back out. There isn't anything about what happened in between." He smirked. "That is, if there actually was anything in between."

I shook my head. My cheeks were hot, my mouth dry. "What about the fuel consumed?" I regretted the words as soon as I'd spoken them.

"Now that's a good question. How much fuel was consumed?" He waved his hand toward my face, and then pulled it back. He bit into the end of his pinky. "There is no way of knowing the rate of fuel consumption inside the hole. Remember, we know virtually nothing about the hole. We don't know anything about what's past the first fifty meters."

"What about the twenty hours I was in there?"

"The on-board computers verified that you were in there for only ten minutes," said Turen.

"What about my cheeks and chin? I had a day's growth."

He tilted his head back and looked at me down his nose. "Where? I don't see it."

I slapped my hands on the table. I rose and leaned across the table, balancing myself on my fingertips. I spoke as quietly as possible. "You're a liar, Turen. It's all there in the recordings."

He grinned. "There's nothing recorded, Artemit."

I smiled. "There is." I stood upright. "I made a copy," I lied, and left the room.

* * *

The next shuttle took me back to Earth. Kitt would take me seriously. I had to meet with her before she talked to Turen.

I pulled out my palm-com and entered her number. She picked up and her lovely face appeared on the screen, but with no trace of a smile. She would take my coming back out of the hole to mean she might have to modify her theory. That was the reason she was not happy to see me, or so I told myself.

"What do you want?" she asked warily.

"It's a long story, Kitt. I really would like to see you. I'll be honest. It's not just that I miss you." I wished I hadn't said that, but I continued. "Things haven't gone

very well since I got back, and I would really like to
talk to you."

"We don't need to see one another anymore," she
said. "Not for a while, anyway."

She was about to close our link, so I spoke quickly.
"Kitt! Wait! There are things that happened that you'll
want to hear about. I can meet you at your place."

"Now?" she asked, her face scrunched up.

"Yes."

She exhaled loudly. "I'll see you when you get
here."

Before I could thank her, she rolled her eyes and the
screen turned black.

* * *

Kitt met me at the door. She wore a knee-length
green skirt with a matching sweater. With her red hair,
the combination was dazzling.

We talked and drank wine while Kitt had her ro-
bots serve spaghetti. I told her about the travel inside
the hole, about the Earths I'd encountered, and I mentioned that I'd seen one or two intelligent life forms.

I knew this was not what she wanted to know.
Since the discovery of the hole, there had been a re-
vival of interest in multiple universes and even time
travel to the past. Kitt and I had both done theoretical
work on this topic. She had developed a theory that
showed time travel to the past was almost impossible.
My theory allowed for backward time travel, but only
through the many universes.

"You've seen some of these other worlds," she said.

"Did you see any evidence that you went to a different time?"

"No. Well, maybe, but I don't think so. All of the worlds I saw had the same Earth and moon as we do. The same sizes, the same distances between them. So if I did travel in time, it could only have been a very short time. There's no way to be certain, one way or the other. In any case, I never went to the past or the future in *our* universe. All the worlds I saw were not the one we live in. That's for sure."

"What do you mean? How can you be sure that you didn't go to a different time in *this* universe?"

"Because of what I saw."

"So what did you see?"

Images of the insectoids flashed through my mind. Slimy, elongated multipedes slithered on the ground. Large, oddly colored creatures, with their spoon shaped bodies, snapped their claws as they lumbered along.

My gaze fell to the floor. I closed my eyes and covered them with my hand. My forehead was wet and clammy. Lowering my hand, I opened my eyes, and —

— I was sitting on a log. There was some kind of grass around my feet. I heard a shrill sound coming from some distance in front of me. Looking up, I saw a purple and yellow insectoid. Yelling, I jumped up, and —

— I was back at Kitt's dining table. My thighs had banged into the table, sloshing the wine in our glasses. I sat back down.

"Jared! What happened?"

Taking deep breaths, I tried to calm myself.

"What happened?" she repeated, as she rapped the table with her knuckles.

"I don't know," I said. "What did you see, Kitt? Did you see anything?"

"What do you mean?"

I opened the palms of my hands, and asked, "Just ... what did you see me do? What happened just now?"

"When you opened your eyes," she said, "you went white. You shouted and jumped to your feet."

My predicament was getting worse: now I was seeing things.

"Jared. Tell me what you saw when you were in the hole."

That was something I didn't want to talk about now.

"Tell me," she insisted, raising her voice.

I picked up my glass and took a deep gulp.

"There was one world. Huge, horrible things, like insects." The next thing I would say, I didn't want to admit, even to myself. "I never tried to find out if they were intelligent. I was too repulsed by them." I drank more wine. "And just now, I hallucinated. It was as vivid as if I was there. I was sitting on a log. One of them was in front of me." I shook my head side to side. "It was so real, it seemed as though I was actually there."

My mind was drawn back to those creatures, and though I was fascinated, images made me shiver.

Then it happened again. Only this time, Kitt was also there. I was again sitting on the log, the shrieking insectoid in front of me, and now Kitt was between that thing and me. She saw the expression on my face and looked behind her. She screamed and moved toward me.

"Jared! Get me out of here. Get that thing away from me."

An insectoid much like a very large centipede started to wrap itself around the bottom of her bare left leg. She cried out, jerked her leg, and dug her fingers into my flesh.

I closed my eyes, concentrated on Kitt's dining room, the table, and our plates, and then opened my eyes again.

We were back. My hallucination was gone.

Kitt was crying, swiping at her tears. She pounded on the table.

"What have you done, Jared? Where did you take me?"

"Where did I *take* you? What do you mean?"

Kitt told me what she'd seen. She had imagined almost the same events that I had!

I got up and went to her, put my arms around her.

She pushed me away. "No. What did you do to me?" she demanded, her jaw tight.

"We had the same hallucination," I explained.

She was breathing heavily now. "No, Jared, I don't think so."

"What do you mean? We saw the same things."

She rolled her eyes. "No. We didn't imagine it."

I stiffened and fought off another shiver. I didn't want to believe it was real. "You think that ... all those things we saw ... were *real?*"

"Yes," Kitt agreed, her long, red hair bobbing.

"There is no way I would imagine something like that so clearly. We both saw the same things. I'm not going back there, Jared. You," her green eyes watered, "have to make sure it doesn't happen again."

"How can I do that?"

"The same way you just did. How did you get us back here? If you know that, then you can make sure it doesn't happen again."

"I concentrated. Hard. Just on this room. That's why we returned." I hurried on. "We need to do this together. We need to keep my thoughts on us, on where we are. That will keep us safe."

"Are those creatures the same as what you saw in the hole?"

I nodded. "Let's put on some music, talk about something different, get our thoughts onto something else."

We went to the living room. As Kitt sat on the couch, I pushed a button and music started to play. I turned back toward her ... and rubbed my eyes.

Kitt had short, straight, brown hair, and sparkling, blue eyes. She was dressed in a bright yellow top and black jeans.

Her smile dissolved. She stood and took a step toward me. She reached for me and put her hand on my shoulder.

"Are you all right?" she asked.

Suddenly, my mind was filled with memories of my life with this Kitt. How we'd met. Our evening together ... the taste of chicken, pasta, and beer lingered in my mouth.

130

Both Kitts, both evenings, both of the lives I'd lived with these two very different women were real to me, *and I could not say that one was more real than the other.*

Nothing frightening had happened here, and I was tempted to stay and just go along with whatever happened next.

But I couldn't do that. This Kitt had been through no trauma. The other Kitt needed me. So, I closed my eyes and concentrated.

Everything froze, and I could neither move nor open my eyes. I heard two different songs, tasted chicken, pasta, and beer, but also spaghetti and wine. One Kitt was asking me if I was all right, the other demanded to know what was happening now. Each had her left hand on my right shoulder, one with a gentle touch, the other with gripping fingers.

I fell to my knees. My cheeks were wet, my breathing irregular. Reluctantly, I opened my eyes.

Kitt knelt in front of me and looked into my eyes. I wished I could dive into those deep, green eyes.

"Where did you just go, Jared?"

I told her.

"Do you still remember the other me, your other life?"

"Yes. They're both real to me."

We were quiet for a moment.

I covered the top of my head with my right hand. "What is happening to me? How can I be going to these worlds that are so different?" I dragged my hand down my face and neck.

"They aren't very different," she said, sharply.

"They're very nearly the same. Think about it. It's not that hard to figure out. Look. All the worlds you went to through the hole were very similar, not different. There was always the same Earth and the same moon. That says to me that the hole connects worlds that are very similar."

She took my face in her hands and looked at me. For the first time that night, her expression was soft.

"Now your mind seems to be connecting worlds that are very similar to you."

"If that is what's happening, when will it stop?" I couldn't help sounding wimpy.

Before Kitt could answer, I was ripped away again. This time I was in a place where I didn't belong. I don't recall much of what happened. I was with yet another Kitt, whose hair was blond, in a lab somewhere. That other versions of Kitt and myself were in a lab made no sense to me. We were both theoretical physicists and there could be no reason to be in an experimental lab. Yet there we were, writing things down, doing some sort of measurements. What I remember most vividly was that, at one point, I turned to look behind me. For an instant, I saw two tall, thin humanoids. I realized I'd seen similar such beings before: the ones that I had dreamed about when I was in the funnel. These two creatures that I now saw alarmed me much more than they should have, dreams or no. They grinned at me, one raised an arm, and I shuddered. Somehow, these creatures meant something very important to me. But I had no idea what that might be.

Then I was back.

"Jared! Stay with me!"

"This world wasn't like the others," I said. "All I know for sure is that I didn't belong there. And I can't remember much of what happened."

As I looked up at her, everything around me melted. Surrounding me was a place that bore no resemblance to our world. It was as if I was experiencing every possible universe, yet was in none of them at the same time. Everything that could possibly happen to me was indeed very real, yet somehow did not exist at all. All of this and more was in my mind only when I was there; I remembered few details after I returned.

At some point, I must have lost consciousness, for the next thing I remember was Kitt sitting by my side. She held a bag of ice on my forehead.

* * *

As the night went on, I learned how to control where I went, how to get back, and how to keep some worlds out of my mind. With each world where my life was slightly different, I acquired another lifetime of memories. Just as one can remember many books and know what material goes with what book, I learned how to distinguish between events in one lifeline as opposed to another.

As I connected with more of the other worlds, I learned of other versions of Kitt and of myself. In some of these worlds we were enemies; in others, friends; and in a few, there was romance. Being a part of these worlds, the lives of other Artemits, helped me to accept things as they were in my world.

The hole is now closed. Somehow my going through

it sealed it off. It is now just a finger of space and time about fifty meters long. Anything sent in now always comes back out, and the study of this oddity has been reduced.

Kitt and I and others still work on our theories, but not so intensely anymore. I have to find some way to prove what I know. I wonder if there is a way to open the hole again, why it was built, and by whom.

The two worlds that don't fit with the others un-nerve me the most. Both of these worlds will not let me in. That is the only thing they have in common. The world in which everything seemed possible, but nothing was real, is one that I am glad to be restricted from. I cannot stop thinking about the other world, the one with Kitt in the lab, and the two strange, thin human-oids.

I doubt that I will ever go near the hole again. Right now, all in all, my life is better than it's ever been, and I don't want to do anything that might change that.

* * *

In his quantum-world, where everything could happen, yet nothing ever did, Belonthar focused his attention on the most likely string of events. He approached the Wise and Aged One. He knelt on one knee, and waited.

"You have news for me."

"Yes."

The Wise and Aged One rolled his hands over one anoth-er. "Have you convinced Artemit to make us real?"

Belonthar hesitated. His eye-slits closed slightly. "Not quite yet." He quickly added, "But we are close. And we have an unexpected new development."

134

The Wise and Aged One swept an arm upward. "Rise and speak of this."

His head bowed slightly, Belonthar said, "The connection we had hoped for has been made. What we had regarded as highly improbable has now become ... remotely possible." His eye-slits widened. "We have a new option to consider."

"Continue."

The fingers on Belonthar's right hand slid over one another. "There may be another. One like our Artemit. A different Artemit. It may be possible that they can be linked."

"Tell me more of this."

Belonthar explained.

Eye-slits closed, the Wise and Aged One thought for some time.

"Pursue this, Belonthar. Focus on our true Artemit, as you know you must. But also find out about this other one."

Belonthar bowed, then left.

There was work to be done.

Double Click

~~~~~~~~~~~~~~~~~~~~~~~~~~~~~~~~~~~~~~~

Jeffery had been waiting for his chance all day, and now that it was finally here, he could not seem to do it. But he had to. He might not get another opportunity.

All the other children were down at the beach. He listened to their shouts and laughter. This would be their last swim before fall. Looking again at Mrs. MacQuarrie, his stomach twitched, and then, seeing Mrs. Phillips sitting on the bench next to her, his ears burned and his legs went weak. He started to leave.

"Jeffery," Mrs. MacQuarrie called to him. "Hello, Jeffery. Why aren't you down at the beach with the other children? Aren't you feeling well?"

For a moment, Jeffery was mesmerized. Mrs. MacQuarrie didn't look like the girls in his grade, or even in the higher grades. She was bright and color-ful. She wore a fuzzy pink top and a black skirt. Her auburn hair surrounded her face in waves and curls. Mrs. MacQuarrie's legs were crossed and her foot gently bobbed up and down. Jeffery's eyes followed.

He swallowed, put his hands in his pockets, and shuffled toward the teachers, kicking loose rocks along the way.

"Why are you here, Jeffery?"

"I ... I wanted to tell you something."

136

Sheila MacQuarrie smiled. "OK, tell me."

Jeffery looked at Mrs. Phillips. She wasn't the same as the girls either, but she wasn't like Mrs. MacQuarrie. Mrs. Phillips was all dressed in white. She touched Mrs. MacQuarrie's knee, and her leg stopped moving. Mrs. Phillips placed the palm of her hand on her forehead, looked up at the clouds, and closed her eyes. Jeffery looked back at Mrs. MacQuarrie.

"It's a secret. I just want to tell you."

"It's all right. Mrs. Phillips can keep a secret."

Jeffery hesitated. He made up his mind.

"I ... I ... I love you, Mrs. MacQuarrie."

There. He had done it. What would she think?

"I love you too, Jeffery."

The boy looked at the small rocks near his runners and nudged one aside. "So then," he said, "would you ... could we ... get married?"

Sheila MacQuarrie smiled but did not laugh. "I'm too much older than you, Jeffery."

He tilted his head down and licked his lips. Then his eyes settled on Mrs. MacQuarrie.

"I'll catch up to you. I'll get older, and then we could get married."

"I'll get older too, Jeffery. So you'll always be much younger."

She sighed, and continued, "And that means..."

It was too late. Jeffery had pulled his hands from his pockets and was running toward the other children.

Sheila watched him as he rose with the hill, reached the top, shrinking as he ran, until he disappeared.

A single tear filled her eye. She wiped it away before Janice Phillips could see it, and they went back to their conversation.

* * *

As he neared the beach, Jeffery slowed down to a quick walk. He took in deep, rapid breaths to try and get his breathing back to normal. Noticing the dampness on his forehead, he wiped sweat away with his hands and rubbed them on his shorts.

"Hey, look guys. It's mister lover boy."

Jason, Fred, and Trip stood before him. Fred and Trip were the same height as Jeffery, but Jason was about three inches shorter. The three of them made a triangle, Jason closest to Jeffery and the other two behind Jason. Except for Jason, all the boys were wearing short-sleeved T-shirts and shorts. Despite the heat, Jason had on full leg-length jeans and a heavy jean jacket, the sleeves coming down a bit past his wrists. He wore a metal chain around his neck. His mouth was in a pout and the rims of his eyes were red.

"Still in love with teacher?" taunted Jason, his arms stiff at his sides, his fingers bunched up.

"I just like her, that's all." Jeffery wiped his palms on his shorts.

Trip and Jason circled him. Jason spoke again.

"Not what we heard … nerd. Ha! Heard. Nerd. I like it. You like it mister lover boy?"

Jeffery followed Jason, turning to keep them face-to-face. He didn't notice where Fred and Trip were. Fred was on his knees and he scurried to put himself behind Jeffery. Jason pushed Jeffery and he tumbled over Fred.

The three boys laughed.

"In love with teacher. Like she's gonna want a nerd like you," said Jason, his finger stabbing through the air, down at Jeffery.

They jogged away, laughing.

Jeffery got up, dusted himself off, and headed back to the beach.

* * *

Sheila looked at the lady in the mirror. She had dark patches beneath her dull, empty eyes. Her head was tilted forward and her face was blank. Her stare was unfocused. In her hand was a bottle of pills. She needed them to help her sleep. But they could serve another purpose. So simple: just swallow them and wait.

She filled the glass with water and raised the container to her lips. She paused, thought of Mick.

He was running after her, chasing her in the warm autumn air. Leaves crunched underfoot as she twisted her way through the trees. She giggled and felt the urgency to stay beyond his reach, with the hope that he would catch her soon. When he did, he took her in his arms and they slowly dropped to their knees. She looked in his eyes, falling into them. His lips pushed against hers, and—

The white bottle of pills still in her hand, she breathed out slowly.

Teaching the children could not fill up her day. If only she could skip these empty times, leap past them. She looked at the bottle again. Could she sleep the time away? No. The prescription would run out too fast.

Sheila put the pills away. "One more day," she decided.

* * *

A package arrived for her the next morning at school. No return address. She waited until lunch to open it. Sitting by herself in the teachers' lounge, she crossed her legs and, almost listlessly, bounced her foot up and down. Oblivious to the other teachers' discussions, she snipped the string and cut open the parcel. Enclosed in bubble paper was a beautiful, burgundy pen. She unwrapped it and put the paper down beside her lunch.

The pen had an uncanny eloquence. It felt ... warm, soft. It settled in her fingers as if it belonged there. It seemed to glow.

Sheila pulled out a sheet of paper to write on. She clicked the pen and glanced up at the clock.

Her fingers froze, the nib of the pen floating just above the table. The clock read 3:40. She looked around the room, but none of the other teachers were there. All the lights were off. The paper, the bubble wrap, her lunch, and her bag were gone. She must, she decided, have fallen asleep.

She walked toward her classroom. As she passed Janice's classroom, she noticed her friend was still here. Sheila knocked and, without waiting for Janice's reply, entered.

"Sheila! We all looked for you." Janice walked toward Sheila and placed her hands on Sheila's shoulders. "Nobody's seen you since lunch. Where have you been?"

"I ... I don't remember. I must have fallen asleep." She pinched her lip between her thumb and finger.

"Asleep? Where?"

"In the lounge."

Janice folded her arms. "No. We'd have seen you. You must have left and nobody noticed. Where did you go?"

Sheila drew in a sharp breath. "I woke up in the lounge."

"But you left. And you didn't take your bag." Janice turned to her desk and picked it up. "Here," she said, and passed it to Sheila.

"I must have ... gone somewhere," Sheila said, shaking her head slightly.

She became aware that the pen was still in her hand. Without thinking about it, she pressed the knob of the pen.

The pen double clicked and the tip went up inside.

She wondered where she had gone and what she had done. How had she returned to the teachers' lounge?

"You've been working too hard," Janice said as she closed her eyes and rubbed her brow with the palm of her hand. She went on, "I told you not to spend so much time marking."

"The children need feedback."

"Not as much as you think. And that's not really why you do it. You work too hard, Sheila." Janice lifted her eyebrows. "What happened today proves it."

Sheila shrugged.

"Get a good sleep tonight. I'll tell the others you're all right."

* * *

This time she would do it. Never mind the happy times they'd had together. That was all gone, in the past, never for her to have again. She looked at the tiny white capsules. Just dump them in and wash them down. She filled the glass. Memories rushed in.

* * *

"Mrs. MacQuarrie? You can go in now."

She joined her husband and the doctor. Mick's eyes were black, heavy. His smile was forced. He held her hand too carefully.

"What is it?" she asked, though she knew, and the doctor told her.

"No. You've made a mistake."

Mick put his arms around her. "It's no mistake, Sweetie. We had good times together, you and I."

"Good times, yes. But only one year." She thought of how they'd met in their first year of teaching, finding out that they'd gone to the same university. Why couldn't they have met sooner?

"Some people don't even get that," he replied.

"It's not fair, Mick. Not fair."

"Never is, Love." He held her shoulder, pulled her tight against him, her cheek on his chest.

She glared at the doctor. "How much time do we have?"

"A month. Maybe two."

* * *

After the funeral, and when the people had all gone

home, she was alone. No one phoned her. Nobody came to visit. Both her parents and Mick's were dead, and neither of them had siblings. There were friends, yes, but the friends that were hers weren't very close, and the close friends were Mick's.

Nothing seemed real. Not a thing mattered.

Except her students.

* * *

She put down the bottle of pills and the glass.

Yes, tonight she would leave.

She couldn't do it right now. Not yet. Not before finishing her marking. The pills would be there when she finished.

Later, almost done, she checked her watch. It was 8:30. She should have had her supper by now, she thought. Supper. No need for any more suppers. Finish marking first. Just one paper to go.

Her pen ran out. She reached in her bag and pulled out another. She clicked the ballpoint out and recognized the musical double click the pen made. It was the pen she'd received earlier today. She almost smiled.

She marked the last paper. Finished, she looked at her watch. It said 11:30. The battery must be low.

All that was left was to record the grades. She wasn't quite ready yet.

By habit, she turned on the TV, went to the kitchen, and put her tea cup in the microwave. She went to set the timer, and —

— the clock read 11:33.

The news was on TV.

It actually was 11:33.

She stumbled back to a chair and sat. Sheila pressed on her lips with her fingertips. What was happening?

After a few minutes, a strange thought occurred to her.

She turned to the weather channel.

The burgundy pen in hand, eyes on the time displayed on the TV screen, she pushed the knob in and heard the pen's double click as the knob went down then back out, and the ballpoint retracted.

Still looking at the TV, she saw that nothing had happened.

She double clicked again, and the ballpoint came out.

It was 2:22!

Double click. The ballpoint went in. Still 2:22.

Double click and the ballpoint came out. 5:38 a.m.!

Sheila MacQuarrie sat quietly, thinking and wondering. She decided to test the pen again, but she'd wait until the teaching day was over. The pills temporarily forgotten, she showered, ate breakfast, and went in to the school.

At the end of the day, she remembered her decision about the pills.

What if...?

* * *

The pen let her jump ahead. Whenever the ballpoint came out she would journey. When it was clicked back in, nothing. She experimented. If she clicked very quickly, she would skip only an hour or so. If she held the knob down, the pen made a single click, then another click as she let the knob come back out, and she found she could travel a long way ahead. One week-end, she went from Friday night to Sunday night on just one double click.

She got used to it. She decided to use it to skip the empty hours that almost drove her to end it all. Soon she had a pattern. She worked Monday, hopped to Tuesday morning, worked Tuesday. Then she slept Tuesday night. She did the same for Wednesday, Thursday, Friday, and the weekend. The pen allowed her never to have any empty time, never to drift into her past. She kept the pen next to her all the time: at school, in bed, in the shower, everywhere.

She didn't speed ahead through time as she dou-ble clicked. She didn't move at a rate of one hour per second, so to speak. If she had, the people around her would have seen her frozen in front of them. No, she jumped—vanishing, and reappearing later—without staying in the same place as time went by for the rest of the world.

One time, Sheila carefully opened the pen. Inside was a golden, glowing cylinder. There was no way to open it. She rolled it around in her hand. Again she felt its warmth, and thought, yes, this pen belonged to her.

She remembered a familiar saying: "Any sufficient-ly advanced technology is indistinguishable from mag-ic." Who would send this pen to her? How? Why?

Time passed quickly. The years started to go by. She was constantly occupied. Though she was very care-ful, she slipped one time, and used her pen accidental-ly. One of the other teachers, Mr. Johnson, noticed that she'd disappeared. Even though he wondered if he'd really seen what he thought he had, he didn't discard it as some trick his mind played.

At the end of that teaching day, the teachers had a meeting. When it was over, he approached her. "Sheila," he called after her as she walked to her classroom.

"Mr. Johnson." She kept walking.

"Would you like to go for a drink?"

"No, thank you. I have marking to do."

"You could do it later."

She was at her door and slipped in the key. He blocked the door so she could not pass.

"Just one drink, Sheila."

He hovered over her, breathing loudly through his nose, his large, right forearm separating Sheila from her classroom. His face was void of expression, except for a faint frown across his mouth. The man seemed never to blink. It was as if he were a statue, except for his noisy inhalation and exhalation.

"Why the sudden interest, Mr. Johnson?"

"I … ah … I always wanted to ask you, but just never got up the nerve." He raised his eyebrows and forced a smile.

"I'm not interested. Please leave me alone." She held her bag close to her chest.

He asked her again.

"Look. I'm telling you, no. Could you just leave me be?"

His fingers closed in on his palms. He turned

around and walked away, deliberately making loud footfalls as he went.

"Glad that's over with," she muttered, and entered her room.

* * *

Jeffery and Jason had their shirt-sleeves rolled up, hands bunched in fists. The two boys were sweating, drops flying off them as they hopped and threw punches at one another. A crowd had gathered to see how this scrap would play out.

"Stay away from Darlene. She's mine, you punk," warned Jason.

"Not yours. She likes men, not girls," replied Jeffery.

The audience offered up a loud "Wooooooooooo!" at that.

Jeffery was momentarily distracted by the gasp, and Jason landed a punch square on his right eye. He stumbled back and Jason hit him hard on the cheek. Jeffery went down and rolled on his back, heels over head, onto the balls of his feet. He sprang up and closed in on Jason. He swiped at Jason, but the boy stepped easily aside.

"She's my girl, not yours," warned Jason.

"She's not yours, except in your one-handed day dreams."

Another moan from the spectators.

"You're gonna get it now, you—"

Jason almost ran right into his opponent. Jeffery backed up as quickly as he could but Jason closed in. He reached Jeffery and swung, landing blows on both of his competitor's cheeks. Jeffery went down. He barely moved.

Jeffery managed to roll onto his side and get up on one knee. After a couple of tries, he was on his feet and went toward Jason. He swung aimlessly.

Jason laughed and punched Jeffery in the stomach, knocking him back down.

Jeffery again rolled onto his side and attempted to stand up. This time he couldn't do it.

Fred and Trip went over to join Jason, and the three of them moved off. The watchers began to disperse.

Jeffery groaned, and stayed still.

Darlene had been well back in the crowd. With Jason gone now, she went to Jeffery's aid.

"Are you coming, Darlene?" asked the other girls.

Darlene looked at Jeffery's bruised cheeks. "I'll catch up with you," she said.

The girls shook their heads and left the two of them alone.

Darlene stroked Jeffery's hair. She cried quietly. "Do you see what I mean now, Jeff? We have to break up for a while. I couldn't stand to see you get hurt anymore."

Jeffery swallowed. "Is that what you want, really? Or … the pressure your friends put on you. It must be hard."

Darlene held back a tear. "That's part of it," she lied. "But we'll get back. Later."

He gasped, still trying to recover his breath. "All right, Darlene," he said at last. "I'm doing this just for you, though."

Darlene kissed him softly on his ear, and whispered, "Let's have one last night together."

* * *

Kissing her deeply, Jeffery pulled Darlene closer. As they touched one another, Jeffery kept having flashes of Mrs. MacQuarrie. Her face. Her eyes. Her legs. The shape of her body.

Guiltily, he pushed the thoughts aside.

They returned later that night just as he fell asleep, and he dreamed of her again. He tried to kiss her, but she gently pushed on his chest. She smiled. "You have to catch me before you can kiss me," she said, and she ran away from him.

* * *

To Sheila's delight, even though Jeffery had long since left her elementary school, and was now in high school, he had visited her quite often and regularly through the years. He'd rap on her door after classes were done for the day. She was surviving after all.

Whenever Mr. Johnson saw her, he gave her the stone faced look that prompted her to cringe. The man wanted something. Mostly, he just looked at her, but there had been one memorable episode.

She'd lost track of time marking in the teachers' lounge after a meeting.

"Hello, Sheila."

She stiffened, cleared her throat.

"Mister Johnson."

"My friends call me Phil."

"What can I do for you … Mr. Johnson?"

He approached and sat down next to her.

149

"Could I borrow your pen please? I forgot mine and I just have to write a short note."

Sheila handed him the pen she'd been using, and started to pack her things into her bag.

"Ah, not this one, Sheila. Could I use your burgundy pen? It looks like a nice pen."

"No. That's a special gift ... from a close friend."

"I just want to—"

"No."

She rose and tried to step past him but he stood up, blocking her exit. He moved closer, almost touching her. She had to step away. He moved right up to her, backing her up against the wall.

"Just let me use the pen. That's all I want."

Squirming, she tightened her grip on her bag. "No. Leave me alone."

He put his hand on her shoulder.

"Stop it!"

His hand slid down her arm, to her elbow. She tried to squeeze past him, but he had her trapped against the wall. He blew out air through his nose onto her face, moved his hand to her hip, and squeezed.

Tears pooled in her eyes.

"Leave me alone. Please."

"All you have to do is let me see that pen."

"Why do you need it? It's just like any other."

"Sure it is." He moved his hand up her side, until it was level with her breasts. "This doesn't have to be difficult. It's up to you. Let me use the pen, or..."

"Stop. Please. Let me think."

"There's nothing to think about. Make your decision."

"Mrs. MacQuarrie, are you all right?"

The voice startled Phil Johnson and he took a step back. Sheila slid quickly along the wall and hustled toward the door.

"Let's go to my office, Jeffery."

Jeffery glared at Johnson, his hands instinctively rolled into fists.

"All right Mrs. MacQuarrie. But if you have any trouble, from anybody, please let me know."

* * *

Later that night, Sheila resolved never to leave herself vulnerable again. She washed her salty face and wiped it dry. Sheila noticed that the lady in the mirror looked different, had some life in her eyes. Her cheeks had some color. Her posture was good: shoulders back, head held high. She bent at her waist and leaned toward the mirror. She noticed that her skin was quite smooth, and the lines near her eyes were hardly noticeable. Yet the other teachers' eyes did have the lines.

Suddenly she straightened and raised her eyebrows.

"I've not aged as much as the other teachers. Thanks to the jumps."

In the past years, she calculated, she'd skipped about sixty percent of the time, and she'd aged about four years.

It would be some time later that the significance of that would become clear to her.

* * *

Jeffery stood outside Mrs. MacQuarrie's classroom door. He looked at the package he held. He raised his hand to knock on the door. He lowered his arm and took a deep breath. Memories of her flashed through his mind. His stomach moved as he thought of all the times she had stood next to him, explaining something, the aroma of her hair … the day at the beach. He smiled slightly to think of all the times he'd stopped by after school to see her. She must know! Did she think that he just—

Don't be a coward, he thought. *Do it.*

Sheila heard the knock and said, "Come in."

The door opened and he stepped inside.

"Hello, Mrs. MacQuarrie."

She looked toward the doorway on her left and smiled. "Hello Jeffery. It's nice to see you again."

He's a young man now, she realized. *Must be twenty-two. Nice guy. Good looking, too.*

"How have you been, Mrs. MacQuarrie?"

"Oh, Jeffery, you don't have to call me Mrs. MacQuarrie anymore. Call me Sheila."

"Hot out today," he said, wiping his forehead.

"Yes. Nice and cool in here though."

He looked down, ran his fingers over his eyebrows.

"How is university?" she asked.

"Good, really good. I've actually just finished all my exams. I'll graduate this year."

Sheila pushed her chair back and swiveled to face him. She crossed her legs, then bobbed her right leg in slow, liquid motions.

Jeffery's eyes automatically traveled up and down her legs. Suddenly aware of this, his ears cooking, he tore his gaze away.

"Has time gone by that fast?" Sheila asked.

"Well, it seemed quite a long time to me."

And even shorter for me, with all my jumps.

"What have you got there? Looks like a gift for your girlfriend."

Why had he come here? "Umm, ah, ... yes. No."

Everything had clicked into place. How could she not have realized this sooner?

"It's not for your girlfriend, is it?"

I'd like it to be, he thought. He swallowed again.

"This is a gift, for you. I ... I mean, I finished off my degree, and I wanted to thank you for all the help you gave me when you were my teacher."

He shook his head, looked down, and meekly passed the package to her.

"Thank you, Jeffery. You didn't need to do that."

"Yes, I did. It's important to me..."

"Can I open it now?"

He nodded, his mouth midway between a smile and a grimace.

Inside was a lovely blue pen. Sheila laughed. She looked up at Jeffery, saw the expression on his face.

"I'm laughing because it is such a beautiful gift. Very appropriate."

She took the pen out and clicked it, wrote on a piece of paper, and smiled.

"Thanks so much. I love it."

It's now or never. No, it can wait until later. No it can't!

"Mrs. MacQuarrie ... Sheila ... would you like to go for a walk? This weekend? In the park, along the beach?"

He knew his face was deep red, and his shirt was probably soaking wet.

Sheila closed her eyes, and thought about his invitation.

"I'm not sure, Jeffery. I ... it's been ... a long time, and..."

"I understand," he said. He waited, hoping something would happen.

They exchanged goodbyes and he left.

Sheila found herself thinking about walking with Jeffery along the beach while she was supposed to be marking. But she pushed it aside, at least for a while.

Jeffery walked home, replaying what had happened many times, never quite satisfying himself, never quite accepting that she'd said 'no,' or perhaps that she hadn't said 'yes.'

* * *

Later, after Jeffery had gone, Mr. Johnson came to her office. He knocked on the door and entered her room. He quickly moved toward her.

Sheila got out of her chair and tried to get away. It didn't work.

"The other teachers are still here," she said.

He pushed up against her. She tried to move away. He seized her wrist, pulling her toward him.

154

"Stop it. Stop now." She tried to scream but her voice failed her.

"Little Jeffery's gone home now, Mrs. MacQuarrie. There's nobody left to save you this time."

He wrapped his other arm around her waist.

The pen. In her hand she held the pen. If she could get her arm free, she could jab it into his shoulder.

She had a better idea.

She slid her thumb up the pen, double clicked the ballpoint in, plunged the knob down, and let it click back out.

Johnson stumbled in the empty space.

He cursed.

After looking around the room, he stood there for some time.

He walked to the door, opened it, glanced back and said, "I'll find you, Sheila."

* * *

Johnson was not there when she returned. She'd feared that he might have come along with her, his hand having been closed around her wrist, but she was alone.

Sheila walked toward where she thought the light switch would be. Taking small steps and reaching ahead of her, she bumped into a couple of students' desks before she found the wall. Sweeping her hands up and down, farther along the wall, her hand finally made contact with the light switch.

She looked around her. No sign of anyone. She had her hand ready on the pen's knob, just in case.

She gathered the students' assignments, put them

into a folder, and turned off the lights as she left the classroom.

Sheila forced herself to move silently out of the building and to her car, and kept searching for any sign of danger.

Reaching for the door, she stiffened as his arms enclosed her.

The bag fell. The pen went skittering across the pavement. Johnson's eyes followed it.

"Nice pen you have, Sheila. How does it work?"

"What are you talking about?"

He smirked. "Don't even try it. You and I both know what it does. I saw what happened that day. You were sloppy, picked out the wrong pen. Thought no one saw. But I did."

She remembered. "No, Mr. Johnson, you're mistaken. I—"

"Back then, I thought it might just be me, seeing things. It bothered me. I knew what I saw, and I watched you. After what happened this afternoon, well, I'd like to try that pen out for myself."

"You're not really after some little pen, are you?"

He laughed. "You thought I was after you? What a joke."

Sheila said nothing, surprised that she felt no relief. She relaxed her muscles, no longer fought his grip.

"So how does it work?" he asked again. His hold on her had loosened.

She drove her elbow back, but he had released her and stepped away. Her arm swung through empty air.

Mr. Johnson now possessed the pen. He grinned as he lifted it off the ground, held it in his hand. He laughed.

Sheila watched him, and her pen, click out of sight.

* * *

Johnson sniggered. He had the pen! He'd figured out what it did. It had pushed her forward in time.

He had plans. Big plans. And now it belonged to him.

He looked at Sheila and laughed.

He had a grip on the pen.

His thumb pressed down.

The pen made a single click.

The knob went in.

It did not come back out.

There was no double click.

* * *

As Johnson and the pen disappeared, Sheila let out a long, agonizing wail.

She looked at her bag and its contents spread over the pavement.

"I'll wait until you get back!"

Then she flopped down and started to cry.

It wouldn't matter how long she waited. He could just jump again, and again if need be, and eventually he'd come back when she wouldn't be there.

"So now you'll have the pen forever," she lamented.

Sheila MacQuarrie did not realize how perfectly correct she was.

* * *

There was nothing to do but go home.

Her marking done, she started her routine to use the pen. It was, after all, a Monday. Remembering that she no longer had the pen, she stopped and stood silently for a few minutes. She walked slowly to the couch, sat, and put her elbows on her knees. She brought her fingers to her lips, then dropped her head into her hands.

Eventually, the tears came. She sobbed quietly for a long time. She leaned back and let her arms fall to her sides. Time slid by.

There was nothing to do. No one to phone. It did not occur to her to watch television, listen to music, or read a book.

Her thoughts drifted back to Mick and she cried again.

* * *

She tapped out some of the pills into her hand, and then noticed the expiry date. She almost laughed. Whatever the chemicals in these capsules once were, they were certainly no longer. Probably she would just get a headache. She threw the bottle into the trashcan.

There must be another way. What about her razor blade? This would work, she thought. She breathed in and out deeply a few times and placed the blade on a prominent vein of her left arm. Her right hand jerked, stopped. Lifting the blade, she saw that she wasn't even bleeding: she'd barely nicked herself.

She placed the razor blade against the vein, pushed it against her arm, and...

...she dropped it into the sink, and looked into the mirror.

Something in those eyes in the mirror ... something showing her...

A smile formed on her lips, her mouth opened, and she laughed. She placed her hands on her cheeks, moved closer to the mirror, peered into her eyes, and laughed again.

She looked down into the sink, gathered tissue paper and, very carefully, wrapped it around the sharp metal object. Satisfied, she deposited it into the garbage, where it belonged.

Sheila enjoyed another laugh. Her fingers ran through her hair, and she clapped her hands together, hopped up and down on her toes.

Sheila MacQuarrie went to bed and, just before falling into a blissful sleep, thought of Jeffery.

* * *

Phil Johnson didn't come in the next day, or any time after that. He eventually became, officially, a missing person.

Sheila herself was late the next day, but she showed up, and did so every day after that.

* * *

Jeffery and Sheila walked along the shore of the lake. It was the end of April and the warm days had returned. Too soon to swim, they had the beach almost all to themselves.

"So, how is the pen?" he asked her.

The pen? Gone. Forever. Sheila smiled. "It's lovely. You shouldn't have spent so much."

"Why not? It's one gift in all these years. Even *I* can afford that."

They talked about her teaching and his studies at university.

"What made you change your mind?" he asked her. "I mean, I'm glad you did, but I..."

She thought about this for a moment. "I took some time to think."

As they walked, his hand brushed against hers every now and then.

He stopped walking and moved his fingers over hers. She squeezed back. They held hands and walked some more.

"Do you remember when I was a kid, and we had that outing at the beach here?"

She grinned. "You asked me to marry you."

He laughed. "Yeah, I did. Pretty gutsy for a kid."

"I told you I was too old for you."

They reached the top of a hill and stopped to enjoy the scenery.

"You said you would always be too old for me."

"I did say that, didn't I?"

She thought about her special pen. She wasn't so much older now.

Sheila turned to face Jeffery, and looked into his eyes. She shrugged and said, "I've changed my mind."

REMEMBERING THE FUTURE

Professor Alfred Turen thumped his right fist into his left hand. It was time to put Artemit in his place. He'd do that tomorrow, perhaps even this afternoon. He checked the time and saw that his meeting with Artemit was to start soon. Already on his way toward the faculty club, he wondered what Artemit had to say to him. He tugged at his ear and muttered to himself. A tall man, Turen's long strides rapidly drew him toward the rendezvous.

Ray Artemit savored another sip of his dark beer, wiped his right arm across his mouth, and smiled as he thought of what he was about to do to Alfred Turen. On the table in front of him were what some would regard as archaic tools for theoretical physics. To Artemit they were priceless antiques. He picked up the stylish burgundy pen, and tilted it to and fro, admiring the glimmer of light that danced off of it. Years ago, this simple device was used for the most sophisticated of theoretical physics inquiries. Artemit hummed as he observed the formation of the symbols that his pen made on paper, developing simple ideas into fuller and more complicated structures. He rubbed his beard absent-mindedly as he checked his conjecture on the containment-field. No, Kitt Wilson's containment-field. What a discovery she'd made.

Artemit's work on backward time travel showed promise. With the pace of technological advances he imagined personal time machines that you could carry around in your pocket, perhaps not in the near future, but someday. An amusing thought struck him: collectors of antiques could one day have their time machines put inside a pen; the knob could be used to select the jump in time. The strange idea made him laugh.

"What's so funny?"

"Ah, Turen, so you showed," said Artemit as he pointed a finger in the air. "Good for you. Not quite as good for me, maybe, because the next beer is yours, and ... here it is now."

Turen sat. They tipped their mugs and mumbled salutations.

"I'm a busy man, Artemit," Turen said as he picked at his ear. "Lots of things to do. What's so important that it can't wait until tomorrow, when your theory will be shattered and mine proven right, when we—"

"Maybe so, Turen. But that's tomorrow. Enjoy your fantasy until then. Right now, I have something I'd like you to explain to me."

For an instant, the corners of Alfred Turen's mouth started to turn up and the slightest twinkle played in his eyes.

Artemit drained his mug, ran his hand over his mouth and beard, and nodded to the server for another.

"What? What can I help you with?" asked Turen.

"Well ... I read your latest paper on Zeno's paradox."

Turen shook his head. "What are you talking about? I—"

"You wrote it using a pseudonym, but the brilliance of the argument gives you away. I have a question."

"Whatever. Suppose it's mine. Ask your question." Turen waved a hand.

"Bear with me first, Turen. See if I've got the paradox right. One way to put the paradox is to say that an arrow, shot toward a target, will never reach the target."

"There are better ways to put it."

"For sure. Let me carry on."

Artemit used his pen to draw a cartoon of the arrow and the target.

"Why do you use that thing, anyway?" Turen grumbled.

"See here," Artemit said, ignoring the jab and rubbing his finger over the drawing. "The arrow leaves toward its target. Before it can get there, it has to travel halfway there. Before it can get halfway there, it has to travel half of halfway. And so on, infinitely. So the arrow can never reach the target. Won't even leave from its initial point." Artemit raised his eyebrows. "Yes?"

Turen laughed. "Crudely put, but basically that's the idea. So what?"

Artemit scratched the hair under his chin. "So, I don't think you can ever write anything about this paradox."

Turen's face flushed.

"Why not?"

Artemit lifted and opened the fingers of his right hand. "Because ... before you understand the paradox, you have to understand half of the paradox, and before you understand half of the paradox, you have to understand half of half of the paradox. So you'll never understand the paradox."

Turen's jaw muscles twitched.

Artemit leaned forward, wagging the pen just a bit too closely to Turen's nose. "If you can never understand the paradox, Turen, how can you write anything about it?"

Before Turen could formulate a response, Artemit drained the last of his beer, tucked his notepad under his arm, stood up, and said, "See you tomorrow."

* * *

Turen walked rapidly from the faculty club building along the path to the physics building, banging his fist into his palm repeatedly. When he reached his office he slammed the door shut. He kicked his chair and threw his coffee cup across the room. When he eventually calmed down, he checked his e-mail. His graduate student had finished the manuscript she'd been working on. He read it. It would be a good publication.

She had put herself as first author of the manuscript. He cut out her name and pasted it after his. He slid a finger across his chin. Before he could change his mind, he sent it to *Physical Review J* for publication.

* * *

"So here it is gentlemen," said Kitt Wilson. She pinched her lower lip. "Here is where it all happens."

She pointed to the tiny chamber within which she had trapped a single electron.

"This monitor shows the probability of finding the electron at a radial distance from the center of the spherical containment field. Also shown are the uncertainties in the position and momentum of the electron. Notice that the wave function is zero at the radius of the containment field." Wilson ran her fingers through her long, dark hair. She went on. "We tell our students that you can't know the position and also the speed and direction of a particle at the same time. There is uncertainty in both, and the product has to have a minimum value. I have found something that ... well, that..." Wilson covered her mouth with her hand and looked down at the floor.

Artemit took a step toward her and said, "You have found an ingenious method which confines a particle within a small volume by using the containment field, the C-field. You've devised a way to generate a C-field by accessing the quantum gravitational aspects of the particle that is inside the C-field." He put his hand on her shoulder. "A tremendous achievement, Kitt."

Wilson's gaze shifted to Turen and Artemit. Turen was tall and thin, and towered over Wilson. Artemit, with his wild beard and wind blown hair, held her eyes for a moment longer than she'd intended. She said, "You each have a theory about how the containment field works. Your theories make different predictions as to what will happen when the containment field is reduced to a small enough size."

She twisted her lip between her thumb and finger,

and paused as if she had come to a barrier, but only briefly. "My contribution," she continued, waving her hands aimlessly, "is that I've developed experimental methods that generate, maintain, and, just recently, reduce the volume inside the C-field, make the field's radius smaller. Small enough that, ... well, that your two theories can now be tested."

Wilson placed her hand on her neck as she regarded the two theorists. "You have different views." She faced Turen. "You, Alfred, predict that the particle's energy will increase sufficiently that the uncertainty principle will be obeyed." She turned toward Artemit. "You, Ray, have made the extraordinary claim that, well, that..."

"That, because of the coupling between the particle and the C-field, the particle's energy has an upper limit, and the C-field has a critical volume," said Artemit. He held his hands in front of him as if he was holding a large ball. "When the upper limit of the particle's energy is reached, which occurs when the size of the C-field is reduced to its critical volume," he moved his hands closer together, "the uncertainty in the particle's momentum can't increase any further. So, when the volume inside the C-field decreases past its critical value..." he brought his hands together so they almost touched.

"The particle will start to disappear," Wilson finished for him.

"Not instantly," Artemit continued. "It will go from being fully in our three-dimensional space, to being partially in our three-space, and then, at a second and smaller critical volume, the particle will be completely squeezed out of our three-dimensional space. It will disappear." Artemit smiled at Wilson.

"Utter nonsense!" said Turen, bringing his hands together in a loud slap.

"Kitt," Turen pressed, "surely you've already done the experiment, and you therefore also know what will happen when you shrink the C-field?"

"No, Alfred. No, I have not." She raised her hands. "Oh, I wanted to, but patience, I hope, will have its rewards."

"How do you mean, Kitt?" Artemit asked.

Wilson began to pace, her gaze fixed on her shoes. She cleared her throat, glanced at Turen, then Artemit, then back at her feet.

"Let's be honest. I know the rivalry between the two of you. Everyone does. Both of you are my colleagues. I simply couldn't take the next step without both of you being here. This is going to crush one of you. I simply couldn't publish a paper saying which of you is right, which is wrong, without telling you first. I decided we should, just the three of us, do this together."

"And once it is done?" asked Turen. He twisted his ear between his thumb and finger.

Wilson pinched the bridge of her nose. "Then we can talk about how to minimize the pain for one of you."

Artemit scratched his beard and said, "I think I understand now, Kitt."

Turen pursed his lips. "So do I."

"There is no way to minimize the pain, Kitt," said

Artemit. "You said to be honest." He pointed briefly at Turen and then faced Wilson. "He can't stand me and I can't stand him. One of us is going down in a few minutes, and the other is going to start partying big time."

"But—"

"No Kitt, he's right," said Turen. "It's true. We've always been enemies. One of us goes down and one of us carries on."

"Why..."

The two men shrugged.

There was nothing to do but start the experiment and see who was right.

* * *

Artemit watched as Wilson reluctantly pushed the button and the C-field started to reduce in size. The monitor indicated that the electron's energy increased as the volume dropped. The C-field's size was closing in on the critical value.

Waving her hands in front of her, Wilson said, "Now the electron will either start to disappear or its energy will continue to increase."

"Its energy will simply increase," said Turen, kneading his right ear.

"The particle will start to disappear," said Artemit, rubbing his beard.

The critical energy was reached. The wave function started to drop: 98 percent, 93 percent, 87, and on until ... the electron fully disappeared.

"There!" Artemit shouted. "It's gone. It's left our three-space and gone to the higher dimensional spaces, just as I said it would!"

"No..." protested Turen. "It can't be. It doesn't make sense."

"It does! Sure, the uncertainty principle still holds, but now you have to take into account the position in the higher dimensional spaces. The momentum too. It's gone, gone, yes it's gone," Artemit sang. "The higher dimensions do exist."

He rushed over to Wilson and wrapped his arms around her, lifting her up, and twirling her around. She couldn't help but laugh.

"It can't be, Artemit," said Turen. "It goes against Newton's laws."

Artemit set Wilson down, whirled around to face his opponent. "*What?* Newton's laws? You're talking Newton's laws in quantum gravity?"

"Well, why not?" Turen pointed a finger upward and it jittered around. "The C-field and the electron exert equal and opposite forces on each other; Newton's third law. The C-field exerts a force inward on the electron, squeezing it into a smaller volume, causing the electron's energy to increase."

Neither Kitt Wilson nor Ray Artemit knew what to say.

Artemit finally spoke, " 'Equal and opposite forces?' It's *quantum gravity* Turen. Not Newton's laws."

"I don't believe this." Turen shook his head. "You're both idiots to believe this stupid result. It goes against common sense. I know what's really going on here."

"What's that?" challenged Artemit.

"You two ... you have ... conspired." He slapped

his hands together. "Do it over Kitt. The experiment. Honestly this time."

"I have, Alfred, I—"

"Do it over!"

"I did it already." Wilson's voice started to quiver.

"Do. It. Again."

Her hands were shaking as she reset the dials and began anew with another confined electron.

Artemit folded his arms across his chest.

The result was the same.

"What is your game you two? Do you think I am so easily fooled?" Turen glared at Wilson. "So help me, you had better do this over and do it fairly or..."

"Or what?" said Artemit. "Are you going to hit her? Beat her up? Your simple-minded theory, your safe approach—that's all you ever do, Turen, take the safe approach—well, it's wrong. Take it like a grown man. Admit you're wrong."

"Shut up, Artemit, or I will—"

"What?" challenged Artemit.

Turen started toward the experimental apparatus.

"Move aside Kitt. I'll do this."

Artemit was about to intervene, but his confidence wavered when he saw Turen pull out a laser-cutter. It could gouge either him or Wilson deeply in half a second. "Are you mad?"

"Shut up, I said." Turen turned toward Wilson, and said, "Last chance, Kitt. No more fixing the results."

Reluctantly, she ran the experiment, and it turned out the same as before.

"That's it. I'm going to do the experiment myself."

Turen stepped forward. His shoe caught something sticky on the floor. He lost his balance and stumbled into Wilson. The cutter went off.

Wilson moaned and slumped to the floor. Blood gushed out of her.

Turen dropped the cutter, covered his mouth with his hands. "No. No. This is not ... I thought it had no power left ... I didn't mean for this to happen. I..."

Artemit placed his hands over the gash in Wilson's chest, trying to staunch the flow of blood.

She coughed up blood and went limp. The spurts stopped, the red liquid now seeping slowly out of her. She stopped breathing.

"No! This is not happening!" Artemit cried. He turned toward Turen ... and everything changed.

Artemit cried out again, but the words ran backward.

Wilson started breathing. Blood crept slowly into her body. She jerked and un-coughed as blood moved into her mouth.

Artemit's hands moved off of Wilson's injury.

Turen un-spoke his last words and his hands moved away from his mouth. The cutter jumped from the floor into his hand.

Blood leapt from Wilson's clothing, from the floor, arced perfectly, and squeezed back into her body.

Wilson rose from the floor, as if gravity had been reversed. She un-moaned. The pulse from the laser emerged from her chest and flowed back into the cutter. Wilson's wound was gone.

Turen un-stumbled and stepped away from her. He said, ".flesym tnemirepxe eht od ot gniog m'I .ti s'tahT" The experiment ran in reverse. He un-spoke again, Artemit said "?dam uoy erA", and Turen put away the cutter.

Time stopped.

No one moved.

No one talked.

Yet time went on in Artemit's mind. Everything that had just happened, or 'un-happened,' had been running forward in time, in his mind. Time should have run backward, but for him it did not.

He remembered the future.

Turen took a step toward Wilson, and Artemit, realizing what was about to happen, lunged at Turen. He twisted Turen's wrist. Turen grimaced and dropped the laser-cutter. Artemit hit him, hard. Then twice more. Turen's face was bloodied.

Artemit heard Wilson calling his name, pleading with him to stop. He shoved Turen away and looked at Wilson.

Turen said, "Move aside Kitt. I'll do this."

Turen went past her and studied the experimental apparatus. Artemit stared at the uninjured Alfred Turen. Wilson acted as if nothing had happened. Speechless, Artemit watched Turen set up the experiment.

The electron was trapped in the C-field. Turen made the field decrease in size. The critical volume was reached, and...

...became smaller. The energy of the electron simply increased. None of the electron went missing. All that happened was that the volume decreased and the electron energy increased.

"So you see, the uncertainty principle is satisfied in our own three-dimensional space," said Turen.

He swiveled the chair and grinned at Artemit and Wilson. "I don't know what you two were up to, but, as you can see, my prediction has been verified. Why did you try to trick me?"

Artemit was barely able to talk. "What ... is ... going on here?" he whispered to himself. Turen was running the exact same experiment that Wilson had, so how could he possibly get different answers? "I don't believe what I'm seeing," said Artemit.

"Well, let me repeat it," said Turen. He did, and got the same result that he'd arrived at before. He did the experiment once more, getting the same outcome. "So much for your conspiracy, both of you, and so much for your stupid theory, Artemit." Turen clapped his hands together, got up from the chair, and started to leave.

"Wait," Wilson called out. "There was no trickery, Alfred. Let me try again."

Artemit watched in disbelief as Turen walked backward *toward* the chair, sat down, and ran the experiment three times, but in reverse. He got up and walked backward *away from* the chair.

Everything stopped again, and it seemed to Artemit that he was experiencing slices of time that were thrust jaggedly together.

Turen said, "Move aside Kitt. I'll do this."

Wilson raised her hand. "No you won't. This is my lab. You are a guest here. Quit questioning my experiments. The results are definitive. They don't support your theory and that's unfortunate for you. I asked you here to give you some time to prepare for the worst, and you repay me by questioning my integrity? There is the door," she pointed, "and it will let you out the same as it let you in."

"What," Artemit asked, "are the results exactly?"

"Pardon? What do you mean, Ray? You saw them yourself."

"Yes I did," he said. *And a lot more than that,* he thought. "Humor me Kitt. What did we find here today?"

Wilson glanced at Turen. He ought to have been upset, but it didn't seem to her that he was. Hesitantly, she said, "We got clear evidence that your theory is the correct one, Ray."

"What!?" Turen exclaimed.

"What did you see, Turen?" Artemit asked, his voice smooth and calm.

"I saw what happened. I saw the electron's energy rise, and it didn't go anywhere."

Artemit eased himself back against one of the lab benches. He crossed his arms over his chest and rubbed his chin with one hand. Only half listening to Wilson and Turen arguing, he thought about what he'd witnessed and what all of it meant. An idea took shape, and he examined it as he waited until Wilson and Turen had nothing further to say.

"So, the two of you see different results," Artemit

said, raising a finger. "You, Turen, say you saw just an increase in the electron's energy. But that's not what Kitt saw. How do you explain that? And don't give me this line of 'You two are in this together.' "

"I know what I saw, Artemit. You two are— No. Wait a minute here. What did *you* see Artemit?"

"Kitt, you saw the C-field collapse and the electron disappear. Turen, you saw the C-field collapse and the electron energy just continue to rise. As tempting as it is, Turen, for me to say that I saw what Kitt saw—"

"Ah, so you come clean then: you acknowledge that you didn't see your theory validated."

"Oh, yes I did."

"Alfred, just admit it. Why fight it?" Wilson, ever the mediator, jumped in.

"Wait Kitt," said Artemit. "I've got an idea. Now bear with me." He took out his pen and a piece of paper. "You've both seen me use this pen, right? So here is what I am going to do. I will write down a prediction. Then I will ask Kitt to do something, I'll say what in just a minute. If I'm right, you can't dismiss what I'm going to write."

"This had better be good," said Turen.

Artemit wrote on the paper, folded it, and gently placed it on the lab bench next to Wilson.

"All right. Kitt, would you show what the computer recorded? Nobody talks until after we've seen it."

Wilson played the recording.

They all watched.

Artemit said, "Turen, you first, then Kitt, then me. What did you see, Turen?"

"What do you mean?"

"I mean that you just saw a replay of the experimental results, and now I want you to say what you saw."

"I saw what I've seen all day: the C-field just got smaller and the electron's energy increased."

"Alfred! How can you say that?" Wilson was undoubtedly exasperated. "*I* saw the C-field collapse, reach a critical value, at which point the electron started to disappear, and when the field reached another critical value, the electron was gone. Why deny it, Alfred?"

"And," said Artemit as he put his hand on the piece of paper, "I saw ... *both!*"

"No way."

"What are you saying, Ray?"

"Here," said Artemit, picking up the paper and offering it to Turen. "Read what I wrote."

Turen took the paper, opened it up, read it to himself, and crushed the paper in his hand. Then he reached into his pocket with his other hand and gave Artemit what appeared to Wilson like a small laser-cutter.

"How ... how did you know?" asked Turen.

"What does it say, Alfred?" asked Wilson.

Turen smoothed out the paper. "It says: 'Turen will see the electron's energy increase. Kitt will see my theory validated. I will see both.' There's an additional sentence: 'Give me the laser-cutter: it still has some power and we don't want any accidents.'

"This isn't possible," Turen concluded.

Wilson nodded enthusiastically. "I agree: it's not."

She pinched her lip. "How could we see different things? How could you possibly see both, Ray?"

He told them what had happened to him.

"Turen, I can't stand you. But... what happened here today... it's huge. We did a quantum experiment. Suppose," he continued, "it is possible that we could get very different results. The many universes interpretation of quantum mechanics would say that the universe would split when we did the experiment, and we'd move along one branch, where we saw one possible outcome. That's what I think happened ... almost. We always assume that *everybody* will move along the *same* branch. But that is an assumption. What if ... well, let me put it this way."

He stopped talking, raised his hands above his head, and clapped them together. *"Both theories are correct!"* he exclaimed. "Given what we each saw, isn't it possible that each of us perceived ... a piece of different universes? The many universes. We can deny it," he went on, "each of us insisting that we got different results in this experiment. If we do that, then this goes out to everybody, and a lot of people are going to reproduce this experiment, and we three will have missed a wonderful and rare opportunity. Or," he tilted his head to one side, and held up his open palms, "we could work together on this. Confidentially, so we're the only ones."

After a moment, Wilson's and Turen's eyes met, and Turen asked, "What do you propose we do?"

Artemit told them.

FORGETTING THE FUTURE

Jay Skyler looked in the mirror. Gradually, he tightened all the muscles in his face. Then he relaxed them. He put his thumbs in his ears, stuck out his tongue, and wiggled his fingers. Stopped. He moved his face close to the mirror and suddenly flashed a wide, exaggerated grin. His face went blank.

"This can't go on," he said to himself. He stared into the sink, thinking, what to do? In the cabinet was his razor. He took it out, put the blade onto his wrist. That wouldn't work, he decided. Nail clippers? Pushing them into the skin on his wrist and twisting them around, he was able to get a vein between the sharp ends. He applied some pressure, the clippers closed a bit ... no good, he thought, would take too long, need to cut too many veins. Then he saw what he needed: the tiny scissors. Opening them as wide as they'd go, he pierced one end into his skin and tentatively dragged the point down the blue stripe. After half an inch, he stopped. He'd managed just a slight scratch. "There's a bigger one at the elbow," he muttered, and rolled up his sleeve. Moving the scissors so that the tips rested on either side of the larger vein, he pushed them into the skin and yelped. His fingers trembled. "Cut it, cut it," he whispered.

What about a note? Surely Bel deserves that much.

He dropped the scissors into the sink. His hand reached for the counter. He staggered backwards and out of the bathroom until his legs bumped up against the bed and he sat. Tears welled up and rolled down his cheeks. Closing his eyes, he started sobbing. His right hand banged repeatedly on his forehead. "Stop! Stop!" He rapped his knuckles on both sides of his head. "Get out of my head! Out! Out!" He choked and coughed. His arms dropped to his sides. "Out … please … out of my head. Out." His legs slipped off the bed and his body tumbled to the floor. Jay cried softly for a few minutes. After that, he remained motionless.

* * *

Incoming signal detected. Sleep mode lifted. Working status initiated. Nature of signal: collapsing shell of photons. Two organic life-forms detected. Initiating superficial scanning.

Receiving signature of primitive thinking. Accessing libraries. Life-forms: human. Confirming distance and time units as meters and seconds. Selecting superior human. Commencing deep scan. Examining incoming photons. Wavelength: approximately pi meters. Speed: approximately 299,704,645 meters per second.

Scanning discontinued. All systems returning to automation. Sleep mode restored.

* * *

"Morning, Sleepy Eyes."

Jay's eyelids lifted just enough to see Belinda sitting on the corner of their bed. He smiled as he thought of Belinda's perfect, hourglass figure and her razor-sharp mind. She was like a rock in the rapids of life's surprises. The smartest thing he had ever done was to marry Belinda. He propped himself up on his right elbow. "Good morn—"

His face fell, his eyes widened. Jay watched his wife as she dressed.

She slipped her left sock onto her left foot.
She slipped her left sock onto her left foot.
She slipped her right sock onto her right foot.
She slipped her right sock onto her right foot.

Jay almost didn't believe what he was seeing. He closed his eyes, shook his head, opened his eyes.

Belinda stood and pulled up her black pants, tucked her shirt in, and buttoned up the pants.

Belinda stood and pulled up her black pants, tucked her shirt in, and buttoned up the pants.

His mouth open, his eyes frozen, Jay stared at his wife.

Belinda turned to face him. "Why are you looking at me like that?" Her mouth was tight. She held her arms crossed over her chest.

"I just had … I'm still having…"

"Having what?"

"It's still happening."

"Tell me: what?"

"It won't stop. It's *déjà vu*, and it won't st— Wait! It just stopped."

"*Déjà vu?*" Belinda's arms relaxed. She sat on the bed. "I haven't had that since I was a little girl."

"When I was a kid," Jay said, "it happened all the time. We called it, 'This Happened in My Dream.'"

Cold fingers touched his neck as he thought about the project and remembered yesterday's work on the artifact.

* * *

Robert Anton was project leader and M.D. for the research group. He sat at the end of the table, Jay Skyler to his right and Bobby Briggs at his left. Jay moved his right forefinger over the tabletop in swift, small loops. Bobby's hands were flat on the table, fingers and thumbs spread wide apart. Anton clasped his hands together. There was a screen on the wall opposite Anton.

Anton rubbed his hands over one another and moved forward to the edge of his chair. "As you know," he said, "seventeen artifacts have been found here, under Charon's surface."

"Seventeen," said Jay. "Prime number."

"Might not mean anything," countered Bobby. He tightened his lips and flipped his right hand up and away. "Why not thirteen? Or nineteen?"

Anton put his elbows on the table, and rapidly tapped his fingertips together. He continued, "We found these artifacts because Pluto and Charon share a double tidal locking, each having the same face always directed toward the other. The main artifact is directly beneath this point on Charon's surface." He picked up a laser pointer and put a red dot on the screen.

"Where are the other sixteen?" asked Bobby.

"Part way down the shaft leading to the main artifact, sixteen tunnels branch away horizontally. Your wife, Jay, is working on a pyramid shaped artifact inside a pyramid shaped room."

"How were they discovered?"

Anton pointed the red dot at the screen. He said, "At this special point, where Pluto is always directly overhead, we discovered a weak, artificial magnetic field on Charon's surface."

Anton paused to look first at Jay and then at Bobby. They both looked back at him but not at one another.

"Now comes the juicy stuff," Anton said. "The numbers."

"The values of pi?" asked Bobby, as he interlaced his fingers.

"Right. The most important artifact is the sphere. It's pi kilometers beneath Charon's surface, connected by a circular shaft, pi meters in diameter. If that isn't enough, a circular screw connects the top of the tunnel and the surface."

Anton waited, and Jay obliged him.

"Let me guess. It's pi meters long."

Anton laughed. "Pi meters long," he confirmed. "When I say pi meters, I mean, of course, to the precision that we can measure." He patted his hands together, almost as if he were clapping, and said, "There are sixteen other artifacts, and a few more values of pi. We've got forty-five scientists working on these puzzles. Let's focus on what you two will be dealing with."

The next slide showed a spherical chamber with a small sphere at its center.

"This innocent looking sphere appears to have a

diameter of pi meters ... from the *outside*. That is, it occupies the volume of a sphere with a diameter of pi meters. The diameter of the room: any guesses?"

Jay did a quick calculation and said, "Pi to the pi meters?"

Anton laughed and nodded.

Bobby's face darkened. "Pi meters, again and again," he said, as he placed his hands palms down on the table and slid them forward. "All these values of pi. It has to mean that the sphere and the other artifacts were left for us to discover. Humans, I mean. It could only have been made recently, within the last few centuries, otherwise the builders wouldn't have known we use meters as our unit of distance."

Jay Skyler slid a finger back and forth across his lower lip. "Yeah. If they were made any earlier it might have been pi feet or pi yards. If they were made before humans evolved to intelligence, we'd just see *ratios* that gave pi, like the ratio of the diameter of the sphere and something else that they left for us, even something as simple as a straight bar."

Anton rubbed his hands together. "You'd think so, yes, I agree, but they left a layer of powdered carbon clinging to the surface of the sphere. The carbon is roughly fifty thousand years old."

Anton's eyes shifted between Jay and Bobby.

"Curiouser and curiouser," mumbled Jay. He patted his cheek a few times with his right hand.

Bobby sat quietly, shaking his head, his shoulders hunched forward. "Doesn't make sense. How would they know we'd end up using meters if they made it fifty thousand years ago?"

"They didn't make it fifty thousand years ago," said Jay as he dropped his hand to the tabletop and moved his finger in quick, tight circles. "They made it after they knew we were capable of space travel in our own solar system. Must have been monitoring us. Maybe they left behind an AI to build the sphere and put the carbon on its surface when the sphere was finished."

Bobby waved his arm in front of him, as if swatting a fly. His face screwed up. "Doesn't make sense. Why monitor us?"

"Watching us makes more sense—"

"Well, gentlemen," Anton interrupted, "this artifact is yours to study, to solve. You're assigned to figure it out. You both think you're hot shots, so that's why this artifact is yours. Since it is the only one directly beneath the screw, we believe the sphere is the key to understanding the other sixteen. I cannot stress enough that you are to work productively together. Any sign I get that this isn't happening and you're both off the sphere and you'll be reassigned, or on your way back to Earth. Either of you have any questions?"

Jay examined the circles he was tracing out and said, "No." Bobby gave a quick, sharp shake of his head.

"All right. To get you up to date, here's what we know. The sphere floats at the exact center of the spherical room in which it was discovered. We have no idea what holds it there. We've tried pushing it and pulling it in every conceivable manner. It won't move. Also, no material particle can enter it. Everything we send to-

184

ward the sphere simply bounces off the surface. Except light. Light will pass through the sphere. You shouldn't be surprised that it takes pi seconds to do so."

"It's packed with space!" Jay exclaimed.

"You don't know that," Bobby shot back. "It could be filled with some material."

"Yeah? If it was just some material we'd already know that."

Anton thumped his hand on the table just hard enough to draw attention. "Look. We don't know much for sure. We think that there's nothing inside the sphere except for space and time, but nobody's sure. There's no physical surface, only a boundary that separates inside and outside. You will solve this conundrum, and you'll do it together. Either of you have a problem with this?"

Anton barely gave them time to answer.

"Good. Now get to work."

* * *

Jay's problems had begun when he'd set in motion an idea that came to him while he slept. He had dreamed that he was an expanding, spherical pulse of light, traveling away from the Sun, spreading himself thinner and thinner until the light collapsed in the eye of an alien on a planet orbiting Alpha Centauri. That prompted Jay to suggest that he and Bobby build a light source around the artifact. Jay's idea was to have a spherical burst of light collapse toward the surface, all parts entering simultaneously.

"Nothing will happen," said Bobby, with a wave of his hand, when Jay first proposed the idea.

"Why not?" Jay had asked, folding his arms across his chest as he stepped toward Bobby.

"Look, Jay, it's just a combination of all the other tests." He raised two fingers and put them inches from Jay's eyes. "We've tried two beams entering from opposite sides." He flipped up a third finger. "Three beams symmetrically spaced within a plane." He waved both hands out in front of him. "This is just a combination."

"It's not." Jay curved his fingers and brought his hands together, as if he held a grapefruit in them. "It's the perfect symmetry," he said, as he moved his cupped hands up and down. "The two beams weren't. None of the tests were spherically symmetrical." His hands parted and he lifted his right index finger and held it in front of his face. "This one is."

Bobby was quiet for a moment, trying to find a weakness in Jay's proposal. Instead, he said, "At least it's got the right wavelength."

"Yeah, pi meters," Jay replied.

Jay's logic worked, and Bobby eventually agreed.

Now they were ready. Everything was set.

Jay surveyed the room. A circular floor had been built two meters below the bottom of the artifact. Equipment for measuring properties of the sphere was off to one side. Bobby was examining the computer read-outs displayed on the monitor. Now surrounding the enigma was a spherical array that would send light toward it and record any light coming back out.

Bobby concentrated on the graphs displayed on the computer monitor.

Jay punched the red start-button.

The pulse entered the sphere.

"Pi seconds till the light comes out," said Bobby. "One. Now."

Jay was right. Something special *did* happen: *none* of the light came back out of the sphere. But there was more.

Jay's mind spun. It was sucked into the sphere. Bit by bit, he left his world, passing through the boundary into whatever was inside. He could not speak or move. Jay watched as the sphere began to shrink. He experienced everything twice. Jay observed the events in the normal fashion. He also knew, simultaneously, what was going to happen.

Suddenly, Jay was outside again and the *déjà vu* was gone.

"Man, did you see that?" whispered Bobby, as he bent at the waist and tapped on the monitor. "The sphere shrank. It's smaller now. Wait." He swung his eyes alternately between the sphere and the monitor. "Now it's getting bigger." He stood straight up. "It's back to its original size."

Jay, mouth open, with a dry tongue, said, "Never mind seeing it. Did you *feel* it?"

"Feel it? What do you mean, 'feel it?'"

"Ah, nothing. Forget it," he told Bobby.

He'd try to do that himself, but it was already too late.

* * *

A few days after Jay's breakthrough, he and Belinda went to what they called the 'Charon Research Station

187

Cinema.' There was a large screen and seating for ten. They were there to see the new movie, 'The War of the Worlds.' This time, the movie was done properly: the Martian invasion was in the 1890s, and followed Wells' book closely. Jay was grinning and squeezing Belinda's hand from the start. Halfway through the picture, he froze. Prickles of heat darted over his face and ears. Everything he experienced was too familiar. He saw the scenes in the show, twice: as he was watching and as he was, somehow, almost *knowing* what they would be. The lines spoken by the actors, he heard twice. His sweating and squirming: experienced and … *remembered?* Unrelenting *déjà vu.*

"Jay. Jay! What's wrong?"

"Uh … nothing. Why?"

"You're squeezing my hand too hard."

"Oh, sorry." What could he tell her? He started to slide his hand away.

She pulled back, caressed his arm gently with her fingertips, and whispered, "Is it happening again?"

"How did you know?"

"I didn't. I do now." She couldn't quite bring herself to smile.

"It's just like what I told you before. It's going on … and on. It won't stop. Everything is double. I even know what I'm saying to you while I'm saying it. I even know what's happening in the movie while I'm watching it."

"Quiet you guys!" someone behind them whispered fiercely.

Belinda barely heard Jay say, "I'm OK. We'll talk after the show. It will stop."

It did. Ten minutes after the movie was over and they were sitting in the café, each with a cup of coffee in front of them.

"Bel, please don't tell anyone," Jay said. He looked down and slowly traced out figure eights beside his coffee cup.

"Why not? It's nothing to be ashamed of. It happens to everyone."

"No. It doesn't. Only children. You said yourself, just a few days ago, that the last time was when you were a little girl. And what's more, for kids, it never lasts more than a few seconds."

Belinda opened her arms, her palms up. "It's all right Jay. People have *déjà vu* a lot. Adults too, not just kids."

"No!" Jay hit the tabletop with a rigid finger. "No way. Not like this." He leaned closer and spoke in a higher pitch. "I'm not talking about something that is just somewhat familiar, what a lot of people call *déjà vu* but isn't really. I'm experiencing this just like we did when we were kids. We *knew* we'd previously experienced what we were doing. It was happening *a second time*. It was as if it *had* happened in a dream. I've experienced it many times now. That morning when you were dressing. Some other times, too. But only for a few minutes each time. And just now, Bel?" He glanced around the café. "I had that go on ... *for an hour.*"

Belinda shook her head slightly. "Maybe other people have had it for an hour too," she suggested.

"No. I don't think so."

"Why not?"

Jay raised his arms at his sides, his fingers spread apart. "*Somebody* would say *something*. It would have to be a rare occurrence for nobody to say anything. If there were other people having *déjà vu* for an hour, somebody would talk. They'd see a shrink. Papers would be published. Word would get around."

"Maybe it happens to a lot of people, but it's not well known. There might be papers about it. Did you try to find out about it?"

Jay peered into his coffee. "No. Not yet. It's just not natural, Bel. And..."

"What?"

"*There's a gap now.* I know what's going to happen *before* it happens. Just a split second, but I know it's there. It started out being simultaneous. Now..." He shook his head. "It's horrible, Bel. I can't stand it. I don't know how to explain it. I'm trapped, manipulated, living out stuff that I somehow know has already happened, or maybe is just about to happen."

Belinda chewed on her lower lip. "You don't have to be upset by it, Jay. Why don't you look at it as something special? If you can know what's going to happen a moment before it does, then that might mean there's more to you than just—"

"Just what? No, Belinda. No." He thumped a knuckle down beside his coffee cup. He banged his knuckle every few words as he said, "There's nothing *special* or *deep* about this. I'm going through hell."

190

People were starting to look at them, Jay's voice having grown louder.

"Jay, I'm just—"

"Let's go home now, Belinda."

* * *

Later, in bed, Jay filled his lungs and blew out the air in a long sigh. "I'm sorry, Bel," he said.

She stroked his arm. "Jay, when did this start? I mean, the first time. Not when you were a kid, but just recently."

He took her hand in his and sat up. "The artifact." He told her what he'd experienced during the collapse of the spherical pulse of light. When he was done, she asked questions and he answered. Later, he asked her, "What was it like for you, Bel? When you were a kid?"

"It was like you said. Like I had dreamed it, as if it had happened before." She rested her head on his chest.

"How do you think it would feel if it lasted for … fifteen minutes, say?"

"I don't know. Maybe not so bad."

"Think about it. Imagine it. Suppose you knew I was going to be saying what I am saying right now. That you knew, just a split second before I talked, you knew what I was going to say. The split second is so short you almost don't have time to realize that you know what I am going to say. I lift my hand. You know I'm going to do it just a fraction of a second before I do it. Imagine that, going on, and on. Never stopping."

Belinda's stomach twitched. She sat up next to Jay

and put her palm on her brow. "That would be so strange. I see what you mean. You have to think about it to realize how it would feel."

"I think I can describe it a little. It's like you know the future, and you forget it, and then you remember it again just before it happens. It's like you're forgetting the future."

* * *

The *déjà vu* lasted longer each time. Three hours. Seven. Ten. Then he had it all the time.

"It's an itch I can't scratch," he told Belinda. "No matter what I do, no matter how outrageous, how unpredictable, I always know I'm going to do it. I'm not living a life anymore. I'm a photocopy. Double vision. Two bells ringing at almost the same time."

Jay raised his bloodshot eyes to look up at his wife.

Belinda bit her lower lip.

* * *

"Dr. Anton will see you now, Jay."

Jay thought through what he'd planned to say.

"How are things, Jay?" Anton asked him. "What do you need?"

"Can't sleep. Can you give me something?"

"Have you tried getting out of bed, reading a bit, waiting until you get sleepy again?"

Jay nodded. "Yes. Tried sleeping on my back, my side, my stomach."

"You worried about the artifact? Progress not so good?"

Jay forced himself not to swallow. "It's going all

right. We've made some progress. I think it *should* be difficult to crack, so it doesn't bother me that we're taking some time to get there. No, I just … can't sleep."

"Are you and Bobby working well together?"

"Pretty much. It's as smooth as you could hope for, I suppose."

Anton rubbed his hands over one another. He thought for a moment, and then said, "I think you should take a break. Take the weekend off. No, you need a break right now. Take the next three days off. It's not much time in the grand scheme of things. I'll give you sleeping pills for three days. Then come back and we'll see where you're at."

Jay was only too happy to agree.

After sleeping that night, he talked with Belinda as she drank her morning coffee. She told him what they had discovered so far about the pyramid shaped object inside the pyramid shaped room. When they'd finished talking about her latest efforts, he saw her to the door and wished her a good day.

He took his sleeping pills and jumped past the morning and afternoon. He had no trouble sleeping at night as well. He did this for each of his three days.

The itch he couldn't scratch happened in the evening hours; everything was dual, and there was no way to stop it.

When his three days were up, he decided to end it all, or at least to try.

* * *

When she'd arrived home at the end of the third day, Belinda called out, "Jay, I'm home." She was greeted by silence, and called his name a few more times as she approached the bedroom. When she got there, she found Jay collapsed on the rug beside the bed. She shook his shoulder slightly. He was asleep. She sat next to him, put his head in her lap, and stroked his hair gently. Still he slept. Belinda had found out there were claims that some people had permanent *déjà vu*, but there was no evidence that anyone knew what was going to happen before it did. She fought off tears. *Got to be strong here. Got to help him.* She knew that his troubles had started with the artifact. She could begin with that.

"Wake up, Sleepy Eyes."

Jay shuddered as he came to. "Hi," he managed. He wondered if she'd noticed the scissors. He stole a quick glance at his elbow. There was just a tiny patch of dried blood.

"Can you tell me something, Jay?"

"What?"

"Tell me more about what happened when you were working on the artifact."

"What do you want to know?"

"Tell me the part about your mind going inside the sphere."

"Well … it just felt like I was … part of me was inside the sphere."

"What were you doing, or thinking maybe, that Bobby wasn't?"

Jay's pulse quickened.

"Yeah, why didn't it happen to Bobby too? Is that what you mean?"

"Maybe. Was there anything special?"

Jay thought back. The sphere of light. It was just like it was in his dream, but collapsing instead of expanding. The key was to send in a spherical shell of light with a wavelength of pi meters. He told Belinda he couldn't think of why Bobby hadn't been affected.

"All right. Tell me again why you think it has to be pi meters."

He sighed. "It's pi meters because the diameter of the sphere is pi meters."

"But everything is pi meters."

"Yeah."

"Why do you think they made all the distances pi meters?" asked Belinda.

"Just so that we'd know the message, when we figure it out, is for us. It's the meters part."

Suddenly, Jay bolted upright. He swiveled to look at Belinda.

"Wait, it's not just pi *meters*. It's pi *seconds* too! That's what's missing."

He got up and ran to the door. "I'll be back."

"What are you going to do?"

But he was already gone.

* * *

"No. No way." That was Bobby's response to Jay's suggested new experiment. "You haven't been here since, what, Monday. I've got something going on here and I'm not about to just stop it and let you take over."

"Bobby, this is it. This is the right experiment and—"

"Maybe it is and maybe it isn't. You wait until what I've got running is done."

"How long will that be?"

Bobby pursed his lips. "Two, maybe three days."

Jay's knees went to jelly. "No, Bobby, I can't wait that long. I need—"

"*You* need?" He pointed at Jay's chest. "It's *us*, not *you*."

Jay had to find a new approach. An idea came to him.

Bobby spoke. So did Jay.

"What's the big hurry with ... you ... Why are you..." said Bobby.

"What's the big hurry with ... you ... Why are you..." said Jay.

Jay had spoken a split second after Bobby. Too soon.

Bobby spoke again and Jay echoed his words. A third time.

"How did you do that? What's going on?"

Jay explained, but only briefly.

"I need to do this now, Bobby. Please. I can't wait any longer, and I promise to explain it more fully later."

Bobby looked Jay up and down. He closed his hands and raised them to his chin. Then he extended his opened palm.

Jay smiled and they shook hands.

* * *

The next day, a mixture of Rubidium and Helium vapor surrounded the artifact. A spherical shell of light with a wavelength of pi meters collapsed in toward the surface of the artifact. Inside the Rubidium-Helium mix, its wave speed was almost exactly one meter per second.

Jay said, "One meter per second. That's what we were missing. The sphere has a diameter of pi meters: that tells us the distance. It takes pi seconds for light to go through the sphere: that tells us the time. Together, they give the speed: one meter per second. The light must have a wavelength of pi meters and has to enter the sphere with a speed of one meter per second. How could I ... we ... miss that?"

"What do you think will happen?" asked Bobby.

"I don't know. Something good, I hope."

* * *

New type of incoming signal. Sleep mode lifted. Working status initiated. Nature of signal: collapsing shell of photons. Two organic life-forms detected. Initiating superficial scanning.

Receiving signature of primitive thinking. Accessing libraries. Life-forms: human. Confirming distance and time units as meters and seconds. Selecting superior human. Commencing deep scan.

Analyzing. Success noted. Wavelength of photons: approximately pi meters. Speed: approximately one meter per second. Human selected for scan responsible for success.

The AI in the sphere all but hesitated, then continued.

Defect noted in human. Nature of defect: temporal duality. Most probable cause: previous scanning. Commencing repair. Continuing. Repair completed.

All systems commencing initiation programs. Working capacity increasing.

Commencing test sequence to prepare for possible opening of gateway.

* * *

Something popped in Jay Skyler's mind. The ringing that had been blaring in his mind for weeks suddenly stopped. The duality was discontinued, the incessant *déjà vu* over.

He would never know why.

Jay Skyler worked on the artifact for months after that. Progress was slow, yet steady. The sphere presented many more tests, and much more difficult ones. The solutions were found. Eventually the artifact gave up its secrets, which triggered success with the other enigmas.

Years later, Jay Skyler would be remembered as the person who had opened the gateway, made the first step that allowed humans to meet the makers of the artifacts, and to move out to the stars.

THE ENTANGLED MAN

It was better when I was Allan Gerrold of no fixed address, a homeless man living on the streets. As miserable as that life was, I'd go back to it, if I could.

My new life began one morning when two men took me away. They simply pulled me to my feet, bound my wrists and ankles, and dumped me in their car. I asked what they were doing and why, and told them to leave me be. Neither uttered a word. Trapped in the back seat of the car, I fidgeted, moved to one door, yanked on the handle, and leaned against it. Locked. I started toward the other door. It opened suddenly and one of the men got in next to me. I raised my arms to try to fight him off. He easily overpowered me and forced a cloth over my mouth and nose. I strained my neck and turned away, fighting until the world dissolved.

When I woke, my wrists and ankles were free, but I was imprisoned inside a room with nothing but four walls, dim lights on the ceiling, and a door. Locked, of course. I had no idea where I was or how far this was going to go, and I would have been terrified at that time had I known.

It was not long until a man and a woman entered the room.

The woman was about my height. Her posture was

upright and confident. She wore shorts and a short-sleeved shirt. Her arms and legs were toned. Her black hair was short and straight, cut around her ears, with a touch of gray at her temples. She looked into my eyes with an unwavering gaze.

The man was huge. He stood with his feet shoulder width apart, hands on hips. He had a prominent jaw and high cheek bones. As he chewed a wad of gum, he looked me up and down, chuckling as he did so.

She looked up at him, then at me. I instinctively took a step backward, raising my hands in front of my face, fingers outward. The man laughed.

They informed me that I would be expected to do whatever they told me and warned me to cooperate. From what I read in their eyes I realized I had best do just that. They took me to my suite. It had all I could hope for and more. There was a large, comfortable bed. A desk. Books and e-books. The kitchen had the best of appliances and the fridge and cupboards were filled with good food. This is where I would live for some time to come, while they molded me into what they wanted.

It began with surgery. They implanted small, sensitive, electromagnetic receptors in my brain. I did not have to wait long to learn why this was done.

They took me to a padded room and we went inside. I pressed on the yielding walls and my stomach turned. The woman had a remote control in her hand. It had two buttons on it, one red, the other green.

"You will experience two things now. You will know pain," she said.

She extended her right forefinger and raised the black box in her left hand. For a moment, she did not move. My hands came up in front of my face, my upper arms flush against my chest. She moved her finger slowly toward the red button, paused, and pressed it. I cried out in agony. My hands covered my head. A searing stab of pain went through my right eye and out the back of my skull, followed by another invasion in my left eye. I collapsed and rolled around on the floor. Then more pain, bursts that flashed through every portion of my body. I got to my feet, stumbled aimlessly, bumped into the soft walls, until I fell and squirmed in misery. After what seemed like hours, the torment finally stopped. I heard the man laughing. He crackled his gum noisily.

Worse was yet to come.

"Now you will experience the opposite. Pleasure." Her face was blank, telling me nothing of what was to come. She put out a finger and brought the remote toward it. Her finger hovered over the green button until she leisurely pressed it inward.

I was immersed in the most euphoric of sensations. I knew nothing but the exquisite duration of pleasure upon pleasure. It was by far the most wonderful I have ever felt. And therein was the horror. When the pleasure stopped, despite my best efforts, I could not help but beg her to do it again. With one knee on the floor and my hands clasped in front of me, I pleaded, "Please. Again. Just once. Press the button." She did not.

"This is how you will feel if you succeed in what we ask," she said. "The pain is yours when you fail."

I was theirs, and I would succeed, not to avoid the pain, but to experience the pleasure.

They taught me many things. They filled my mind with knowledge: history, languages, physics, mathematics, mythology, and some of the darker subjects that I would learn to hate. They put me through extensive training that put me in top physical condition. This training went on for weeks, maybe a month. I lost track of time. They never answered any of the questions that I asked them. Why had they chosen me? What were they preparing me to do? Finally, the day came where I started to learn more about their intricate plans. They began by showing me the mice.

"Look closely, Gerrold," said the man, "and tell us how these mice differ." The woman stood back, away from us. She was quiet and still. I studied the mice. I compared every feature. I could see no difference and I said so.

"They are, in many ways, identical. This one is the original. This other one is a copy."

"Cloning?" I asked.

"No. Better." He fell silent and stared at me.

I asked, "What is the copy, if not a clone?"

"It's purely artificial, free of organic matter," said the woman.

Before I could ask, the man said, "Watch what happens." He put the artificial mouse in a container and placed it in a dim corner of the room, some distance from the organic mouse, which was in another container in a dark corridor. He placed an unlit lamp in front of the organic mouse.

"Watch what the artificial mouse does when the light is turned on."

When he snapped the light on, the artificial mouse jumped backward!

He repeated the process three more times. Each time, both mice recoiled at the same instant.

Then he put the lamp in front of the artificial mouse. Again, both jerked in response to the sudden burst of light.

I asked what had happened.

The man said nothing. I looked at the woman. Her back was straight and she held her head high. Her eyes bore into mine and I had to look away.

"You'll find out," she said. I knew I didn't want to know.

The next day they showed me the body. It was on its back, on one of two platforms that were side by side. I was allowed to examine it thoroughly. It was purely artificial, wholly mechanical. On the outside, it was an exact copy of me.

The man put his hand on my shoulder and squeezed until it was almost painful.

"Lay down on this platform," he said, and he guided me downward. He turned toward a control panel, glanced back at me, smiled, and turned a dial. My hands and feet were clamped down. A smooth cup moved upward to support the base of my skull. Soft but firm material emerged from the cup, slid around my head, and held it fixed. Several curved slabs moved toward, and enclosed, my head.

"Surrounding you are several sensitive sensors. We

will use them to scan and determine the state of your brain. The quantum state, of course," he added, almost as if it were an afterthought. "A similar array of transmitters is now positioned around your other brain."

"The information from the scan will be copied into your mechanical body," said the woman. "The state of the artificial brain will be a duplicate of yours."

The man moved toward me. He brought his grinning face close to mine. I looked at him through a gap between the slabs. "And then, Gerrold, you know what comes next, don't you?"

"What?" I asked, my voice small and squeaky.

I could barely hear him as he whispered, "We will then link the two brains together."

It took a moment for me to understand what this linking might mean. My pulse quickened and beads of perspiration formed on my upper lip. "Noooooo!" I cried. I squeezed my eyes shut, as if that might protect me.

I heard the humming of a machine, and it seemed to me that thousands of long, thin, sharp needles stabbed my brain as it was being probed. After a brief silence, there was a buzzing at the other body. The sensory pads moved away. Then three things happened at once.

I opened my eyes and saw the room around me.

I opened my other eyes and saw the room around the other me.

And, to my horror, I was in *both* bodies, seeing with two pairs of eyes and hearing with all four ears. I was simultaneously aware of the perceptions and thoughts in both brains and bodies. Yet there was a single entity, a single me, with one mind.

My wrists, ankles, and heads, for both bodies, were free. My two bodies sat up slowly. What I saw from each was only slightly different, yet my heads swam, trying to make sense of the two images and two sets of sounds. The room swirled around me. I eased back down and closed all four eyes.

"What have you done to me?" my voices croaked. In my natural body, the sound of my natural and artificial voices speaking at the same time, registered in my natural brain. In my artificial brain, I heard this strange, unsettling mixture of two voices. I decided I would speak using only my organic tongue.

"You have been given a great gift," said the man. "You can experience the world from two bodies, with two of everything."

"I don't want this. Why have you done this to me?"

"You'll find out soon enough. I suggest you start learning how to handle your increased awareness. We won't let you lie quietly forever. You'd best get a grip." With that, they both left, and the two of us were, or I was, alone.

I thought of the mice. They each sensed what the other saw. The mice were their last test before changing me.

Why had they done this? A possibility occurred to me, and I shuddered at the idea. I had to gain some control of the strange duality that had been forced upon me, and I couldn't afford the luxury of time.

I closed my artificial eyes and made my new body lie still. Then I sat up slowly, and was aware of doing so in both brains. With the two bodies switching roles, I repeated the process a few times. *I can handle this*, I told myself.

With both bodies lowered down, I opened my pairs of eyes, and slowly raised my backs off the platforms. My heads spun again, but not as badly as before. Fearing their return, I forced myself to adapt. It was a terrible struggle, and I can give only a crude analogy of what it was like.

Think of watching your image, reflected twice, off two mirrors, so that you see yourself as others do. You try to turn your head to your right and tilt it downward. At first you move your head in the wrong direction. With practice, you learn to compensate. What I had to learn was more difficult. The fear of their return hampered me but pushed me as well. They wanted to use me for some purpose. I knew I was in far more danger than I could imagine.

After a time, I learned how to control the two bodies with two brains and one mind, at least to some extent. I was exhausted. I needed to sleep, not just because I was weary, but because I needed to escape. My two brains, two bodies, and one mind were just too much for me to handle. If I could sleep, I could be at peace.

I slowed my conscious thinking, set my mind to produce random thoughts, and drifted, my awareness in the two bodies merging into one. I knew sleep would come.

Instead of escaping, finding some release in sleep, I entered an experience almost beyond description. First there were the inky blue, purple and yellow splotches, and fuzzy blobs of entering sleep. Gradually, I became aware of faint sounds. They gurgled and swirled, and were now too easily heard. The volume grew. Many voices and other sounds mixed together. I heard the screams of slaughtered animals, the cries, pleading, and begging of tortured souls, the maniacal laughing of killers, the shrieking of vast numbers of evil entities. I tried to push the noises away. Instead, the number of voices increased and the voices grew louder. Many more distinct, evil sounds assaulted me.

I descended further into this world, and the purple and yellow blobs took form. Frightening shapes. I saw and felt the presence of terrifying demon-like figures. Walking, decaying bodies. Next came more monstrous forms and shapes. Colors. Reds and browns of blood. Yellows of pus. Blues of bruises. Greens and grays of decay. Evil sounds and more and more horrible visions. Louder and louder. More and more vivid. As disgusting as these were, they were nothing compared to what I was soon to smell, taste, and feel.

Next came sensations: spiders climbing up my legs and arms, snakes slithering, vicious insects attacking me. I felt bites, sharp needles puncturing every piece of my skin. Stabs of pain in my lips and on my tongue.

Smells tortured me. The stink of filth smothered me. Scents of rotting flesh, noxious odors, and the smell of death. The stench of my burning skin and muscles as flames rose up around me. And tastes, of the worst things you can imagine.

I do not want to convey any further the images, scents, sounds, tastes, and sensations of evil and repulsive things I experienced. Of things I knew or had conceived. Many of them more horrible than I had ever imagined. These built and grew until there was no more room in me for horrors such as these. At some point, my mind must have shut down, for I recall a stretch of blackness, silence, nothing.

Then I woke and heard the screaming. My throats were raw and sore. I broke down and sobbed. I shook and trembled. Eventually, I reached a stunned state of mind, and both bodies lay still, and I waited until I had regained control of my thoughts and my bodies.

I knew I must never again sleep, yet that was impossible. There would be no escaping this nightmare. I tried to think rationally. They would not want me to have to endure these nightmares, for if I did, I would not be able to do what they wanted, whatever that might be. I thought I would be used for war. That's what having control of two bodies must have been all about. Having finished with the mice, they had made me a tool for war. They could send the artificial me into enemy territory, and use my original form to report what I would observe. Exactly how they would deploy my two parts, I wasn't sure.

Eventually the man returned and I told him what had happened. He listened carefully and made me report every detail.

"What you have described agrees with everything we recorded," he said.

I realized that they had simply moved out of sight, and had watched everything I had dreamed. I asked how they had known what I'd experienced.

"The implants, Gerrold. They're capable of more than inducing pain and pleasure."

Both of me sat up and I put out both sets of arms in front of my chests, my pairs of hands opening in pleading gestures. "Can you stop this from happening?" I whimpered. "It will interfere with what you plan for me." I tried to put my heads in my hands. My movements were awkward, but I finally managed this simple task. He said nothing, so I raised my heads to see what he was doing.

He looked at the two of us with a blank face. He scratched a tooth with one of his fingernails. "No, it won't affect our plans," he said.

"Yes it will," I insisted. "Look, I realize what you intend to do with me."

He asked me what I meant and I told him.

"I'm your next step after the mice," I concluded.

He turned and stared into my eyes, and his grin widened. He threw his head back and burst into laughter. "You have it all wrong, Gerrold. Sure, you're our next step. But you're not the step after the mice."

"What do you mean?"

"There were plenty before you," he said simply.

"Plenty of what?" I asked. "Of intermediate steps?"

"No. Plenty of people. People who had their brains copied into duplicate bodies."

I swallowed. "What happened to them?"

"They experienced what you did."

"And then what?"

"They died," he said. "You are the first one to survive this long."

My hands were shaking. I could no longer quite bring them under control. "Well, you've got to make this stop. I won't be able to do what you want me to if I have to go through this every time I sleep."

"Again, Gerrold, you've got it all wrong."

He stood and started to pace, looking at one of me and then the other. He hooked his thumbs into the belt loops of his pants.

"Your thoughts in these two brains, in these two bodies, are entangled."

"What exactly do you mean?"

"You know about this. We taught you this."

My legs were also now starting to shake slightly. I concentrated hard, commanded them to stop, and they relaxed a bit.

He breathed in slowly and exhaled quickly. He put his hands on his hips and swaggered in front of me.

"It's like the quantum entanglement of two particles. Pairs of quantum particles can be put into a special state in which the pair of particles can be inherently connected, and remain so even if they are far apart. What happens to one affects the other. This is because the true state of the pair cannot be thought of as two distinct, single-particle states. The two particles together are actually one thing. It's a two-particle system, not two single-particle systems. This special two-particle state is called quantum entanglement."

He paused, surveyed the two bodies, and then continued.

"You saw the mice. They are entangled. Two bodies, but only one ... oh, call it a sense of awareness. You're special because you have consciousness, intelligence. Simply put, there is only one of you. Your brains are innately connected. You're literally the sum of two parts and more than the sum. You're a new type of man. You've gone to a place where no one has been before. No, that's not quite right. You're the first person to go there and come out of it alive."

"By the place I've gone to, you mean what I ... dreamed ... when I, we, slept?"

"Yes. This is a new realm of power, the darker side. We intend to learn how to make use of this power. You," he pointed at my two bodies, "will be our link to this power. All you have to do is sleep. As much as you can. That's what we want you to do."

I tried to swallow. My mouths were dry. I could barely control my trembling limbs.

"What are you saying? You expect me to experience again what I just did?"

He nodded.

"No. I won't do it. I couldn't stand it. It's of no use to you. You can't possibly make a connection to what I just went through."

"We already know how to make the connection. What do you think we were doing while you slept?

You'll do it again." He stepped closer. "And again."
His face moved close to one of mine. "And again, and
again," he taunted. "You know what will happen if
you don't," he finished, as he pulled back and slipped
a small, black object out of his pocket.

I looked at the remote. He dangled it in front of my
bodies, twirling it around, tossing it from one hand to
the other.

The pain I could feel from the little box was nothing in comparison to what I'd just gone through. No
amount of pleasure would convince me to do it again.
I lost it. We lost it. Both bodies charged him.

He pushed the red button down, and easily side-
stepped both pairs of lunging arms.

The intensity was tenfold what they'd used before.
No matter how strongly I willed myself to drive into
him, to tear him apart, the pain was crippling. My two
bodies fell and writhed in anguish. "Turn ... off ...
please..." we gasped.

He chortled. He let the torture continue.

I was thinking of ways that I could escape when,
suddenly, the pain stopped.

Later, with both bodies resting on the platforms, I
heard the man and woman arguing. I couldn't make out
what they were saying. My mind went numb again.

When they returned to the room, they both looked
at us. The man took his hands off his hips, stopped
chewing his gum, and whispered something in her
ear. The woman recoiled from him and glanced at me.
She stepped between the man and me, lifted my arm,
and put two fingers on my wrist. She looked at me, the

original me, intensely, focusing first on my right eye, then on my left eye. She continued shifting her look rapidly from one of my eyes to the other. Then she released my arm, turned around, and walked up to the man. She said something softly, and walked out. He looked at me, grinned, and was gone.

"Stay awake," I said aloud, to myself. "Stay awake."

* * *

They sent me to the hellish place many times. I was assaulted through my five senses, like the first time, each time more intense than the last. They forced my natural body to exercise and kept it in good condition. They could not do the same for my mind. Sanity ebbed with each episode. All I did was exercise, eat, and sleep. I could not fight the sedative they fed directly into my blood stream. They also did something to put my artificial brain to sleep. Routinely, they sent my mind to sleep.

With one exception. One time they'd somehow failed to put my artificial brain to sleep. I remained awake. My natural brain slept, and I was aware of my dreams and also of the room around me. I did not go to the repulsive world. I doubt that it is somewhere in our domain of space and time. It is in my mind, in my consciousness. With every visit, I sensed evil entities. I believe the place is real, even if confined to my mind. If I could be forced to go there, so could anyone else. Never did I see any evidence that they were acquiring any power from the horrible realm, but they kept at it so long I think they must have found something.

After so much agony, I wondered how long it would be that I would retain any shred of sanity. I couldn't help but wonder if this place was the hell that people believed in. If it was, could there be someplace else that was the opposite of this one? I like to think so.

I went through this horror so long that I'd almost lost hope. Then I remembered something, and I vowed to hang on as long as I could.

* * *

"I've put your artificial body asleep. I need you to be very quiet for a while. I'm going to give you a mild sedative. It will relax you, but it won't put you to sleep. Not quite. You have to hang on, Gerrold. Stay awake."

I have a vague recollection of what happened after that, although there are missing pieces and I wonder how she managed it. But she did. Later, well away from where I'd been, the sedative wore off, and my artificial brain woke up as well. I read the message she'd left. She said that it had gone too far for her. With the others, death was always quick, but they learned more from each victim. They hadn't expected me to last as long as I did, and after witnessing my pathetic and horrific experiences so many times, she couldn't go on. So she had saved me and fled. She did not want to stay with me because if they found her, she could not endure what they would do to me next or what she knew they would do to her. She wished me well and advised me to stay where I was.

* * *

I have lived for several years on this atoll. It has

plenty of fresh water, fruit, and vegetables. I only sleep one body at a time. For sixteen hours each day, only one of us sleeps, and we are well. The other eight, we are both awake. We perceive what each other does and thinks. Although we have grown differently, I remain a single person. I don't plan to leave the atoll.

One of us will die eventually. It will probably be my natural body first. What will happen to my mind, I do not know. I live with the fear that they will find me. I hope they are not looking for me, and if they are not, I pity the poor soul who now goes through what I did. Mostly, I am grateful to be alive and not to have to go to that place ever again. I also hope she is well, and safe, that they never find her. I wish I could thank her.

I understand how it is that I have two bodies and one mind. It's what the man said: the pairs of quantum particles exist, not as two single particles, but as a single, connected entity.

The connectedness is also true of me.

I am one person, not two people. I am the entangled man.

CALCULATIONS

\\

"Come in," I muttered, hearing the knock on my office door. I pressed on with my work. My elbows were on my desk, and my hands cupped around my eyes as if holding binoculars. I focused on the detailed calculation I was pursuing, a problem that had baffled me for over a month. I've been a Professor Emeritus in theoretical physics since I turned sixty-five, and now I teach only one course each year. I have the time and the freedom to dig into more exotic puzzles. This particular one had fascinated and frustrated me to the limit.

I'm not sure how much time went by before my guest said, "Professor Ledgier?"

"Yes, yes. What can I do for you?" My door was behind me and to my left, so I hadn't seen who had come to my office. I finally turned my chair to face her. Her eyes were raw, with broken blood vessels lying every which way. Her shoulders sagged and her face was pale. What had happened to this young woman, and why was she here to see me? I rose and wheeled the visitor's chair toward her, in the corner near the door. "Please, sit," I said, beckoning her with my hand. "Make yourself comfortable." I stepped back to my seat. "Are you one of my students?"

I thought I saw tears in her eyes. She placed one

hand over her mouth and looked down. As she sank into the chair, she shook her head. She held a folder close to her chest. "No," she replied. "My boyfriend was in your course. That's why I'm here."

I sat down and pulled at my mustache. "I don't understand. Why doesn't he come himself?"

Her eyes slid slowly toward me. "He can't see you right now. Maybe later."

She dabbed at her eyes with a tissue she had been holding, swallowed, and gently cleared her throat. She raised her head and her sore, red eyes told me she had been through some exceptional experience.

"What can I do for you?" I asked again.

She reached into her folder, hesitated, and withdrew some papers. "I think these will be of interest to you."

I reached out and she placed one end of the papers in my hand. I waited a second or two until she reluctantly let go. Despite my curiosity, I took the material almost reverently into my grasp and looked down at it. There were several sets of notes, all physics calculations. Each had a staple in the upper left corner. I put them on my lap. I picked up the first set, brought it close to my face, and read the title and summary. I lowered the notes and glanced through the pages. They were filled with advanced, difficult calculations. The work was tidy, meticulous, in small handwriting. I put this one on top of the paper I'd been writing on, and looked through the second exposition. It was of the same high quality. I placed it on the first one.

When I picked up the next work, I barely noticed

that all those beneath it tumbled off my lap onto the floor. I held it up and focused my attention. The title. The equations. The method. My right hand shaking slightly, I pushed my glasses up the bridge of my nose. "No, this can't be."

"What?"

The fingers of my left hand pressed hard against my palm. My fist was shaking slightly. "Did he steal this?"

She stiffened. "What do you mean?"

"This work." I flapped the pages through the air. "This work is *my* work. How did your boyfriend find my work?"

She shook her head. "Your work? Why do you say it's yours? He—"

I raised my trembling hand. "He stole my work! How did he do that?"

Her eyes narrowed. She leaned forward. "He didn't steal anything. What makes it *your* work?"

I rolled the hairs of my mustache between my finger and thumb. "I think up problems like this one. Nobody does that as well as I do. No one else even knows that this problem exists! So there is no way your boyfriend could have gotten it unless he got it from me. Or from my office. Or..."

The young woman's shoulders were shaking slightly. Her breathing was ragged. Unable to hold back any longer, her hand covered her eyes as she began sobbing softly.

I reached past her and swung the door almost shut. Sitting again, I started to give her a reassuring pat, then withdrew my arm and clasped my hands on my chest.

A moment later she was calm and spoke firmly.

"I know ... *for certain* ... that he did not steal *your* work or anyone *else's!* "

How could he have done this work? Here was my calculation! Exactly the same one that was sitting on my desk. If this work was truly his, then he had done what I'd been trying to do for the past month. No way could I accept that. I had not even formulated the problem properly. In these notes, though, he had done it all: defined the problem precisely, found the correct method, and carried out all the steps. His final result was exactly what I had expected myself.

My voice softer now, I leaned toward her and asked, in a whisper, "Your boyfriend did this work?"

She nodded.

"All of it?"

"Yes."

"But ... I mean ... if so," I lifted my hand and moved it in a circle, "then he should show this work himself."

"He can't do that. Not now."

"Why not?"

She interlaced her fingers and looked at the floor.

"What would you like me to do?" I asked, opening my hands in front of me.

"He told me that you are fair, that you wouldn't take credit for work one of your students had done. So, I would like to ask you if you could look at his work."

She stopped abruptly.

I cleared my throat and pushed my glasses up. "I'm sorry for what I said. Perhaps this work, all of it, even the one that ... that I said was mine ... perhaps it is all his."

Some life came into her eyes. She spoke quickly. "Could you look at these calculations please? All of them?"

"Just a moment," I said, and scooped up the notes from the floor. There wasn't much room on my desk for them. There were piles of calculations and books covering almost all of the desktop, so I put the papers on my lap again and flipped through them. I could see that these were outstanding works. I shook my head side to side.

"What's wrong?" she asked.

"It will take some time for me to look at all of this. I can get some others to help me —"

She half rose from her seat. "No!" She sat back on the edge of her chair. "No others. Please. Just you. If you find that the work is sound, then..."

"Yes?"

"Then ... could you see that he receives credit for it? That it's published? With his name only? Please?"

"All right," I said, tugging at the hairs on the back of my neck. "These problems, calculations ... they're very detailed. Complicated. It will take time."

"Is it interesting work?" she asked.

"Very."

"Then please take whatever time you need. I'll give you my phone number." She looked for a piece of paper as she tapped a finger on her chin. I pulled a sheet from one of the piles on my desk and gave it to her. She wrote the number and handed it to me. "Please call me when you can tell me something."

She suddenly stood, said goodbye, and quickly left the room.

I hustled to my doorway and called after her.

"Wait, please. What's your boyfriend's name? Who does he work for?"

She turned around, walked back to me, and whispered his name in my ear.

My eyebrows rose, and I nodded to myself as I watched her leave.

*   *   *

As I sat in my office the next day, I thought more about his work. With my hands tucked under my chin and arms against my chest, my eyes roamed over the walls. There was a picture of me and my Ph.D. supervisor, the famous Wilton Somners. It helped me remember what I had achieved under his direction. I smiled as I looked at the pictures of my wife and our children. There were posters of some of the best work I had done in my career. I had a pile of paper on my desk that I had written my calculations on, and on top of the stack were the student's computations. What to make of the young man's work? The papers were written in a style beyond the graduate student level. The words, the explanations ... were too well done.

The collective content of these papers made them quite valuable, I realized, just before I heard the rustling of clothing from someone at my door.

I didn't get the chance to invite the person in. As I

turned to face the door, I saw someone dressed in black wearing a hood and mask that hid all but the person's eyes. I also saw the gun in my visitor's hand. The outfit looked ridiculous, and I almost laughed.

An electronic voice said, "Do you have the papers?"

"What papers?"

"I know all about them." The person waved an arm through the air. "I know you have them. Are they here?"

I opened my hands. "I don't know what you're talking about. Why the cloak and dagger stuff?"

He, or she, closed the door. The electronic voice spoke in a lower volume.

"Don't play with me. I've brought this" — the gun wobbled — "and I mean business. I'll have the papers." The gloved fingers rapidly waved toward and away from me, in a demanding manner. "I'll have them *now*. Get them."

My thumb moved over my mustache. "Ah, well, I have only two of them." As soon as I'd said it, I realized my error: for all I knew, this strange person might not know there were many more, might have believed me if I'd said, 'Yes, I have both of them.'

"Give them to me."

This would be my only chance. I slowly started to peel off the top two sets, pretending they were mixed with my own notes.

"What's with these two papers anyway?" I asked. "It's physics, theoretical physics. It's not like you can sell it on the street."

My intruder stepped closer. That made it more difficult for me to do what I wanted to, but I tried nevertheless. I turned my back to block from view the emergency button by my phone, and reached to press it.

A bang roared in my ears, and I realized I'd been shot. My shoulder. Hot blood squeezed through my fingers, which had instinctively covered the wound.

The shooter kicked my chair and the wheels rolled me away. I watched as a hand reached over my desk and took all the papers, not just the top two. My uninvited guest cut the cord on my phone with scissors, and turned to leave.

"Please! Call emergency," I pled.

The assailant was gone.

* * *

The next day, my wounded shoulder tended to and my phone repaired, I lamented that I hadn't made copies.

The wound on my shoulder wasn't all that bad: the gun was just a pellet gun. No one heard the bang: there hadn't been one. I'd just imagined it.

I went to my office and wrote down everything I could remember that was in the first two papers, and made a rough outline of some of the others. I'd also been lucky to have left one of his calculations at home, and I think you can guess which one.

Now someone else possessed the student's other eleven advances in physics.

I decided to talk about this with my colleague and friend, Jeanne, a Professor in English. I dialed her number only to find that she was also on the phone, so I simply walked over to her office and rapped on the door.

"Come in," she called out.

"Hi," I said and went in.

Jeanne was sorting through various books and materials on her desk. She swept her hair away from her face and behind her ear. She looked up at me and said, "I just phoned you. Did you get my message?"

"No. What is it?"

"Listen ... the strangest thing has happened."

"What's that?"

She glanced around her and picked up a thin, yellow binder. "A student came to see me yesterday. She dropped off a bunch of stories." Jeanne turned the binder in her hands. "She said they were written by her boyfriend. Wanted to know if they were publishable. I glanced at a couple and then started to read some of them."

I asked her the names of the students.

She told me.

My mouth fell open, but no words came out.

"The stories deal with your research area, and there are some pretty interesting ideas. I'd like to know what you think of them," she said, and handed them over to me.

"Here's what's so odd about this whole thing," she added, running her fingers through her hair. "She said to tell you that her boyfriend wrote all the stories in addition to doing all the physics calculations. Does that make any sense to you?"

I shook my head dumbly and left with the stories.

I'd somehow forgotten why I'd gone to see her.

* * *

The handwriting was unmistakable. It was his. As the young woman had said, he'd been in my course, and his handwriting was very neat, with small, crisp letters. I hadn't quite noticed his handwriting in the physics calculations: I was too immersed in the concepts and methods. There was no doubt in my mind now, after having read the stories. He had indeed written the calculations and the stories as well. It was clear to me who had come in disguise to my office to take the calculations away from me. You think you know a person…

I couldn't bear the thought of telling the young woman that I'd lost her boyfriend's work, and I vowed that I would get all of it back.

I picked up the stories and read the titles one more time. They all fit together. Everything made perfect sense.

He had done all the calculations, written all the stories, and in such a short time. Well, a short time for all of us, I reminded myself as I recalled the title of the first story: 'The Quiet Room.'